CAGE ME

CLAIMING KRISTOPHER

Angel Jendrick

Book Four

Formatting: Love Hard Publishing

Cover Art: Quinn Ward

Editing: Savvy Fox Author Services and Allister Thompson Editorial

This book is dedicated to anyone in the world who is currently lost, feeling like they fuck up at every turn and they just can't find their place. Take it one day at a time, and don't ever give in to the madness.

I hear you.

You are not alone.

"Love is so short, forgetting is so long."
- Pablo Neruda

Foreword

Chapter 1

New York City, January 4, 2019

"RAM HER! PUNCH HER in the sides, Corey!"

"Use your feet!"

Courtney, a.k.a. Corey, received yet another bare-knuckle blow to her head, temporarily and quite successfully scrambling the insides of her brain. The spectators forming a circle around her and her opponent faded away until all Courtney could see were the fluorescent lights above her as her back was pressed into the cold concrete floor. And all she could hear were the breathless grunts of exertion as she and the other girl — AMaze — struggled to overpower one another. She was pinned to the ground, her free arm swinging at her opponent any chance she got. AMaze currently had the upper hand as she had Courtney straddled with her knee pressing Courtney's other arm into the concrete. "You have some seriously fucking kissable lips," she gasped just as AMaze struck her in the face again, but she didn't break eye contact with her opponent. She grinned, tasting blood as she added, "I'll try not to hit you in them."

Temporarily distracted, AMaze's gaze widened as she stared down at the mischievous look on Courtney's face; it was enough to weaken the other girl's grip on Courtney. With a tenaciousness that must have come all the way from her toes, Courtney slipped her trapped arm out from under

AMaze, and quick as lightning, she grabbed her wrist before she could strike again. In one, two, three rapid successions, Courtney jabbed her free fist into the girl's forearm. Her opponent's thighs slackened their death grip on Courtney's ribs, and she gleefully saw an opening to get out of the trap she lay in.

Instead of striking AMaze's arm once more, Courtney raised her fist high and tight, slamming the girl on top of her in the eye and again in the head. It worked; AMaze swayed to the side, just enough that Courtney could nudge her the rest of the way off with her knee. She jumped up, already falling into her defensive stance and waiting to see what the other girl would do. She could vaguely hear the shouting from the sidelines — who the crowd was cheering for she couldn't be certain, and honestly, she didn't give a shit about that. A need for popularity wasn't how she'd first ended up throwing punches in an underground fight club many months ago.

Aware blood was spilling from somewhere on her face, Courtney shook off any discomfort and rounded on her opponent. AMaze was looking at her differently now; Courtney's compliment was throwing her off-guard a bit. She enjoyed having such an effect on people — her impulsivity often gave her a considerable advantage.

"Wanna get together sometime?" Courtney asked as they squared off in the ring. She bounced lightly on the balls of her feet, looking for an opening to strike. They traded punches, jabbing mostly toward the upper torso and getting an occasional low kick to the shin or thigh.

"I take it that's a no?" Courtney spoke again, slightly out of breath.

AMaze gave her a dirty look. "Stop distracting me with small talk, Corey. You should've hit on me before the match."

"Very true." Courtney side-swiped another kick before elbowing her in the chest.

Blood, some fresh and some old, marred Courtney's white-and-green Nikes, and as she raised her right foot and swung into a match finale roundhouse kick, she knew more was yet to come. Sure enough, when she connected with AMaze's face and the girl's nose started to gush a red stream, Courtney's shoelaces got covered in the sticky substance.

She felt nothing but numbness as her opponent crumpled to the concrete. When AMaze didn't get back up, the ref announced Courtney the winner, but all she could feel was a coldness seeping into her as she slowly closed in on the loser. She removed her mouth guard and jutted out her free hand to help the woman up. "You're a good fighter."

"Yeah, you too," AMaze muttered, courteously embracing Courtney in a customary hug. Even bloody, with sweat pouring down her face, AMaze was nice to look at. And as she lingered a moment too long in Courtney's arms, it was clear the attraction was mutual. She was no doubt waiting for Courtney to sweep her off her feet, but it was never gonna happen. Courtney didn't understand it, but in those few moments during and after the fight, she'd changed her mind. She pulled away from AMaze, politely saying goodbye before they went their separate ways.

There was a lot of commotion from the crowd, a couple guys even joking that her auburn hair made her a feisty scrapper, but Courtney paid them no attention as she searched for Dagger. It was time for her prize money, and unlike the previous life she'd lived, she needed every coin of that six hundred.

WHEN SHE GOT HOME — just a small room she rented above a bar deep in the heart of New York City — she climbed the fire escape stairs to the private entrance. She kept the hood of her sweater over her head for two reasons. One, she didn't want to draw attention to herself this late at night, and two, if she did draw attention, she didn't want it to be because it looked like she'd been in a fight. Living above the bar and bartending there, anything could have happened, and the last thing she needed was some nosy do-gooder getting in her business. She glanced around, searching for no one in particular as she got her keys out. All the same, she did this every time she came home, constantly on high alert for anything or anyone who didn't seem to blend in on the sidewalk around the bar. It was how it'd happened before with her best friend, Drew. One minute they were laughing, a crowd of marathon spectators pushing against them, and not even five minutes later she was gone, lifeless and riddled with stab wounds as her infant daughter wailed in her carrier.

Without a sound, she let herself into the unit and closed the door behind her. All that illuminated the cozy space was the soft glow from the bedside lamp, and Courtney didn't bother turning on the main light as she locked the door behind her. As she was closing the curtains, movement on the sidewalk caught her eye. A figure by the streetlight stood there, deep enough in the shadows that she couldn't see their face. A chill raced through her as she realized she'd seen him some other time, last week maybe. How had she not noticed him when she'd done her shoulder checks before reaching the apartment?

What the fuck was he doing out there this late, creeping in the dark?

There was a bench a few feet behind the light, she knew from walking past it on her way home enough times. Maybe he'd been sitting and just stood up. Courtney cleared her throat, closing the blinds tight and double-checking the two locks on her door. It was probably nothing.

She dropped her duffel bag beside her feet, immediately heading to the bathroom to fish out her bottle of ibuprofen. She twisted on the sink tap, popping two capsules in her mouth before taking a drink from the running water. Next, she reached for a clean facecloth on the shelf above the toilet and turned on the hot water tap this time. While waiting for it to get lukewarm, she carefully washed her hands, feeling the sting as blood from her skinned knuckles mingled with the water. She yawned, now soaking the cloth under the water and wringing it out gently before dabbing it over the cut on her eyebrow.

Courtney had been in enough fights over the last five months to guess without turning on the light what her face might look like. What was the use? It wouldn't change what was, and she knew from the slowing flow of the blood that her eyebrow wouldn't need stitches. Staring at her battered reflection would only lower her self-esteem even more, and truly, who needed that shit?

After the cut was clean, she washed the cloth out with soap and wrung it well before hanging it over the bathtub. Next, she took out her contacts, dropping them into a container with solution. It took a moment to find her glasses, even after she caved and flicked on the bathroom light. They were nestled between two folded towels sitting on the top shelf of the organizer behind the toilet.

"Faack," she muttered, grimacing at her reflection as she moved in front of the mirror again. Although her face didn't look as awful as it had in the past, it still wasn't pretty by any means. Her normally unblemished ivory skin was swollen around her eye, her cheek, and along her jawline. The bruises there gave the impression she'd been in some sort of domestic dispute, and she briefly questioned how effective her foundation coverup would be.

She incredulously shook her head as she grabbed the bottle of rubbing alcohol, unable to believe this was her new norm. She ran the antiseptic solution over her hands and dabbed some on her eyebrow. When she was all finished, she shut the light off and limped out of the bathroom in the direction of the fridge. Retrieving the open bottle of Merlot tucked between the cheese and the eggs, she was kicking off her battle-worn Nikes the same time she was uncorking the bottle. As soon as her socked feet touched the floor, a nagging pain raced up her leg from her calf. She winced, taking a few swigs of wine before filling a glass close to the brim. No stingy pours here.

Fuck, she was getting stiff, and she knew it was because AMaze had had an annoying preference for leg shots, especially the hips. Even though Courtney had won in the end, the other girl had been a tough opponent. Without setting the wine glass down, she pulled a soft-gel ice pack from the freezer. She dropped it on the counter before wrapping it in a dishtowel and heading to the sofa. She was exhausted now and yet not at all eager to sleep. She knew what awaited her in her slumber, and she'd much rather reminisce with pictures than with a nightmare.

Sipping her Merlot, she traded her ice pack for her old cell phone lying on the cushion beside her, still there from the last time she'd viewed the contents. The phone was no longer hooked up because she'd wanted a fresh start in every way possible when she left B.C. But as much as she wished it, she couldn't bear to part with the memories on the old device. She took another drink, placing the glass down on the end table, and picked up the ice pack once more as she scrolled through her photo gallery. Tears misted, doing a swell job at clouding her vision, but searching the gallery for her best friend's face was practically an addiction at this point. She'd done so every morning and night for eight long months, and she had no plans of stopping.

Drew's joyous face laughed up at Courtney as she baked cookies in the Matheson kitchen, her long, wavy, naturally golden locks thrown atop her head in an efficient yet messy bun. Courtney couldn't remember what they'd been laughing about; to be honest, they'd spent a lot of their time together laughing and genuinely being worry-free. Sure, they'd had their share of problems — who didn't? — but even with the complications Courtney had gone through with her parents, and Drew had suffered with her bulimia and then her father's death, there'd been love and laughter. Lots of laughter.

Courtney sniffled, carefully swiping her thumb over the screen to the next picture. She swapped out her ice pack for her wine again, absently sipping and swallowing as she soaked up the next image. It was of Drew with her daughter Cadence and fiancé Kris. It was actually one Courtney had saved off Facebook, which Drew's grandmother had taken while they'd been visiting her ranch. They were sitting on a picnic blanket in front of two large cherry blossom trees, baby Cadence tucked into the crook of Kris's arm. They looked so happy, finally truly content with life. They could never have known it'd all be snatched from them weeks — not months, not even years, later.

Eventually, while reminiscing, Courtney polished off her wine and nestled down farther in the sofa. She dozed off with the warming ice pack still keeping her eyebrow company and the phone clutched between her fingers.

I spin around, catching sight of a dark figure dressed all in black, a hood obscuring his malicious features. A long, serrated hunting knife drops out of his sleeve, slipping into his hand as if it's a custom fit. He stalks Kris silently in the crowd, slipping through without a sound, and no one is the wiser.

The cloaked assailant suddenly stops in his tracks, and I'm trembling as he slowly turns in my direction, as if he, above anyone else, knows I'm watching.

He lifts his face toward me, and I scream.

"Drew! No!"

Chapter 2

"C'MON GIRL, DON'T QUIT on me now," Courtney panted out as she pulled her body into yet another sit-up the next afternoon. She was still sore from her illegal, no-holds-barred and no gloves match with AMaze, but if she didn't force herself to strength-train each day, the next fight could be brutal. Besides, she doubted pro athletes lazed around and wallowed in misery the day after whatever obstacle they'd endured. The loose idea she'd had of hooking up with AMaze was laughable now; she could just imagine the two of them trying to fuck each other, beat all to hell. Sure wouldn't be sexy.

From her point of view on the floor, staring in angst in front of her with sweat pouring off her injured eyebrow, the misery was winning out today. She was struggling past her second set of twenty, frozen at number nine. When she'd woken at half past eleven, she swore she could feel every single place she'd been kicked the night before. She'd reached twelve throbbing points on her legs and torso before losing count, and when she'd hobbled to a stand, she witnessed the mess in the wall mirror. She'd fallen asleep with her cargo pants and zippered sweater overtop her sports bra, but sometime through the night, she'd taken off the bulky material. Her body resembled a Smurf's as the bruising covering most of her stood out against her pale ivory skin.

Courtney heaved a sigh in defeat on the floor, such a minuscule action making her ribs spaz out in a WTF-are-you-doing comeback. She closed her eyes, lying on the floor for a moment and listening to her heartbeat slow as she caught her breath. What *was* she doing? Since discovering the underground fight club here in the Big Apple, she'd wormed her way into the secret life even without the aid of a manager. She'd fought ten times, quickly becoming a fan favourite since the selection of female fighters barely registered compared with the males. She'd fought the same five women, losing almost as much as she won. With her experience in kickboxing, the organizers of the club set her up with other kickboxers, but she knew a few of them had other martial arts under their belt. Quite often, Courtney felt unskilled in comparison and worried one day it would cost her in the ring.

She was lost since Drew had been murdered, it was true, but she wasn't suicidal. Fighting relieved so much more than just her anguish; it also calmed her racing pulse and the need to run away. It was how she'd landed in NYC in the first place; she'd bolted from Vancouver as soon as the funeral was over. She'd spent a couple of months making her way across Canada, not really knowing what she was headed for. It wasn't until she'd crossed the border and landed in NYC that she eventually discovered something worth sticking around for.

She took her time sitting up and then pulling herself into a standing position. She took a glass from one of the two cupboards in her rental and filled it with water and ice. Downing the cold liquid in four big gulps, she set the glass down and immediately got started on making a low-carb lemon martini. It was one of her preferred go-to drinks since she'd been there, and she supposed it was the same thing as her old phone she couldn't toss away; she'd been making pretty drinks since she was of age. Working in a biker club, as she was now, no one would be caught dead ordering a drink like that. And she was pretty sure the owner didn't even sell all the fancy liqueurs and syrups.

She pulled down her shaker bottle and got some more ice to put into it. Next, she added vodka, unsweetened lemon syrup, and squeezed out half a lemon before giving the bottle a good shake. Taking a chilled martini glass from the bottom of her fridge, Courtney took a piece of the other lemon and ran it over the rim. Then she carefully rolled the rim in her container full of sugar.

"Making these is so much more satisfying than passing out beers to hairy-ass men," Courtney murmured, grinning as she gave her shaker one last mix-up before pouring the contents into the martini glass. She garnished her masterpiece with a lemon slice and headed into the bathroom to start the tub. Work came soon, and she needed a good soak to go with her drink before that happened.

COURTNEY GAVE A NOD to the bouncer, Darius, as she hurried into the back door of the bar that evening. She was forty-five minutes late, which was a record even for her, especially considering she lived directly above the bar. She'd been just walking out the door when she'd banged her split knuckles on the trim. Her hand had started bleeding again, and it'd taken her some time to stabilize the wound. Then, since she couldn't very well go to work wrapped in bandages, she'd had to find a store close by that sold biker gloves. So now, instead of looking as if her AB negative might drip into a customer's whiskey on the rocks, she was rocking this tough-ass biker chick look.

She spotted her boss coming out of the kitchen when she approached the bar counter. He looked agitated. "I don't wanna hear any fucking excuses comin' out of your mouth, Corey; just get behind the bar and let Lou go home. You owe her pay for two hours for covering your ass."

Courtney brushed past him. "Sure, Lee, no problem. And uh, I'm sorry." She went to set her purse down, but he grabbed her arm, effectively training her eyes on his pissed-off brown ones. The color wasn't an exact shade of Kris's, but with those and Lee's unruly black hair, he kind of reminded Courtney of her friend when she was feeling alone.

He must have felt her tense up, because he dropped his hand away, instead watching as she shrugged out of her long jacket to expose her skin-tight leather pants. His gaze travelled the length of her slowly to the functional yet sexy black-zippered pumps on her feet, to her long, athletic legs encased in leather, to a tight black tank top short enough to flash her pierced navel. Plus, now she had a sweet pair of gloves, so the only part of the charade she was losing on was her mass of red curls. As much change as she embraced into her new life, ridding herself of her trademark couldn't possibly be one of them. Besides, with her skin tone, she'd look odd as fuck with black or brown or purple hair.

"Do you need something else, Lee?" Courtney asked when it seemed as if whatever he'd plan to say got as lost as his attention clearly was. He was hung up on her legs, which was fine, if he was checking her out from across the room and not trying to have a conversation with her. She was wearing leather pants, after all; she expected people to desire her in those — it was why she'd bought them. She thoroughly enjoyed teasing people with ideas of sex. She relished the power over them it gave her and quite possibly made her a little sick in the head.

Lee finally glanced up at her, his pissed-off eyes now fired with desire. In her previous life — where the hardest thing she'd done was come out as bisexual — she might have even entertained the thought of giving them what they both needed. He wasn't too much older than her twenty-three, and good-looking in a feral way — huh, now that she thought about it, Lee really did remind her of Kris. Realizing *that* killed her attraction some, but only slightly because she was human, after all; a woman who hadn't had sex since she'd left Vancouver. Despite the fact she'd hit on AMaze the night before, she was on a soul-searching journey, not whatever Lee was hoping for. It left her with little time to bed anyone, and *especially* not her boss.

"I was gonna say your coverup isn't working on your face tonight, but I have a feeling no one is gonna care." Lee was muttering so low, she was half reading his lips.

His words sank in, and she grinned. "Just what I was going for."

He left, and she relieved Lou behind the counter, apologizing for being late. Lou, short for Louise, was a mid-thirties, Harley-driving, leather jacket-wearing classic stereotypical lesbian. She wore her brown hair buzzed short, showcasing the many rings taking the lobes of her ears hostage. She quickly thrust her hand out to shake Courtney's, in the process sliding her jacket sleeve up. Courtney got a glimpse of the tattoos wrapping around her forearm and biceps.

"Don't mention it, Corey," Lou said, turning to grab three beers out of the cooler. She served them to the group leaning against the countertop before coming back to her. "Max is still cooking in the kitchen, so I was gonna grab a beer after my shift anyways."

Maxine was Lou's partner, a stout woman with spiky hair and tats seeming to be everywhere, including her face. The crowd in the bar looked intimidating — hell, they *were* intimidating, but none seemed to bother Courtney since she'd stumbled into the place months ago. She'd proven she could fight when a sleazy guy grabbed her ass and yanked her down on his lap in front of his buddies. She'd broken two fingers on the hand staked around her, stomped on his foot, and elbowed him in the face. When she'd jumped up, he'd been swearing and had his face craned toward her. She'd seen the opening, and she'd taken it, punching him in the throat before kicking him in the chest. His chair had toppled over backward, and when Courtney stopped her attack, she'd realized the entire bar was staring at her. She'd felt senseless and overreactive in the moment, but it'd landed her a home and job. Thinking back on it, she suspected she'd reacted so strongly to being manhandled because of witnessing such violence to Drew. Her killer had been a next-level sociopath, a rapist and murderer, and had only known them because Kris had been stupid and careless. To grow up and befriend ... no, *defend* someone like Dobie for so many years ... in Courtney's mind, Kris had done everything but enable his childhood friend. As payment, Dobie had taken away the most important person in Kris's life.

In all their lives.

Squaring her shoulders and trying desperately to rid herself of her disconsolate memory trip, Courtney got to work behind the bar. As she served Miller and Blue Ribbon, Busch and Budweiser, and rounds of rum and whiskey, she couldn't help but think she'd picked the best place in the world to get lost in. She rarely saw a person with their smartphone in their hands; instead, people played pool and darts and used the slot machines. She was working under the table and using a fake name, in part because yes, she'd wanted a new identity when she left B.C., but she was also so tired of letting people in. Either they let her down, or she did the letting down. She wasn't a person a nice girl or guy should ever give their heart to because in the end she'd just crush it. Her ex, Natalie, knew that better than anyone. So, giving them her real name was just another way they could inch their way past her defenses, and yeah, fuck that. Apart from a minor disguise when she went shopping, she'd stuck close to the bar for the sole reason of no one recognizing her. She'd been in NYC for five months, and no one had identified her from her father's company. It was refreshing to be invisible.

Courtney heard shouting over by the doors, lifting her face from the cash register in time to see a stool breaking across the back of a burly biker. She rolled her eyes at how cliché the assailant was and watched in bemusement as the victim who'd broken the chair lifted the other guy easily off the ground.

She left the counter long enough to shout into the back kitchen, "Lee, Tony and Sal are at it again! And it's not even midnight," she added dryly as he came rushing out.

"Bunch of drunken assholes, always breaking up my fuckin' bar," Lee grumbled, heading past her and signalling to the bouncer by the side exit.

Courtney shook her head and went back to her next customer, all the while keeping an eye on things in the front. Sometimes they escalated, and when that happened, she had to make sure the patrons across the counter from her were free and clear. It was entertaining and immature at the same time, and she thoroughly enjoyed the scuffles most nights. It made her shift fly by, and she was damn certain none of the frat boys in Kitsilano had ever started a brawl like these boys did.

A tingling sensation went down her spine, just as it had the night before, and her Spidey sense went out of whack as she pulled another four beers from the fridge. She couldn't explain it, because she was in a room filled with people buying drinks from her and checking her out, but out of nowhere she felt like she was being pursued. She stood frozen for a minute, wary of who'd she discover behind her and how they'd found her. It couldn't be Kris, could it? Last she'd heard, he was still lost in a catatonic state in the psych ward. Dobie was in prison, unless he'd escaped somehow.

She was deeply aware of her stomach clenching from the sudden nerves. Her palms were sweaty now, and for a millisecond, she fumbled with one of the Budweisers in her hands. Her brain kept going back to last night, to the shadowy figure lurking under the streetlamp.

"Christ, you're three feet away from the fridge, Corey. Don't tell me you're too damn lazy to go back for a second haul?" She heard Lee behind her, shaking her from her thoughts. Their gazes met, and he frowned. "I've known you for five months and never seen you sweat. You feeling okay? The foundation is slipping off your face, you know that, right? Looks like a mud mask got splashed with water; fucking sick."

"Fuck, no, I didn't. Sorry, boss," Courtney replied, wondering if he was about to send her home. She was shaken the fuck up, and now that her makeup disguise had completely worn off, she'd be getting curious glances at her face, no matter how superb her legs were.

He started taking the beers from her hands, returning them to the fridge for colder ones. Sure enough, he said over his shoulder, "I'll finish this up. Go home and take care of yourself."

"Copy that," she muttered, waiting until he'd left her standing there, and still, she didn't move. She was slow turning around, casually scanning the patrons closest to the bar as she picked up her purse and jacket. No one stood out to her as she scanned the many faces, but when she headed to the side exit, she noticed a tall, muscular figure heading toward the front doors. He was ill fitted to the scene, standing out in jeans and a blazer; Courtney knew instantly he'd been watching her. Nerves had the pulse in her throat racing, but she said *the hell with it* and took off out the side door to cut him off at the front. When she reached the sidewalk, the mystery man was nowhere to be found. Mostly puzzled and a little apprehensive, she peered through the tinted windows of the bar, trying to see if he just hadn't left after all. Nothing, nada.

Who the fuck *was* he? And why was he tailing her?

Chapter 3

46th Street, NYC

"NOT GONNA DANCE?"

Courtney glanced up from her apple martini to the vividly out-of-place guy who had come up beside her. He looked too casual and out of place in jeans and a half-buttoned plaid shirt, too country in his cowboy hat, and, well, if she were being honest, too straight.

He gestured to the seat beside her. "May I?"

She turned back to her drink, lifting it off the bar counter to take a sip. "Free country, cowboy."

"Cowboy?" He glanced down at himself like he just remembered what he had on and laughed. "Oh, that. I'm a stripper; I'll be heading up on stage in a few."

Courtney sent him a bored look, not really wanting to be hit on tonight. She'd come with Lou and Maxine but currently had no sweet clue where they'd disappeared to. Maybe there was a hidden card game with high stakes in the basement or something, because the flamboyant club scene didn't suit their personalities at all.

The man signalled the bartender before running his fingers through his short, bleached blond hair. He was okay-looking, if she were even looking to hook up tonight. Which she wasn't. Even if she didn't have a freak keeping tabs on her, she still wouldn't be interested.

"I saw you over here all lonely and shit and thought you might like some company. You're way too gorgeous to be in a club by yourself."

Courtney scrutinized him and wondered what his game was. A stripper who picked up hot girls in their twenties could be just that, a player, ticking women off like board game pieces. Or he could be gaining access to vulnerable women to drug, kidnap, and sell them. Anything went when it came to shady assholes. He didn't look as big as the man stalking her, but that didn't mean he wasn't working with him.

She raised her index finger and made a show of circling the room. "Gay club, remember?"

"You don't look like a lez to me; but even so, I've got ways of changing a pretty lady's mind."

Courtney scoffed, rolling her eyes and taking another drink. "Just how does a lesbian look, dickwad? You looked like a goddamn gentleman at first glance, but you're no more gentleman than I'm into you, so fuck off."

His hand rested on her shoulder and then had the nerve to trace the outline of her bra strap sneaking out of her tank top. She hadn't even bothered to dress up tonight, which wasn't her at all; or at least it wasn't the old Courtney. Maybe this new and improved version didn't fuss over details?

She looked down at his hand, and then up to his face, memorizing every detail in case she needed it later in a police lineup. "Take your hand off me before I fucking break it, pretty boy. I'm not lonely and do *not* want the attention you're offering. So get lost."

The guy recoiled from her threat, and she appreciated the fact that he took it as one. It wasn't that she couldn't be approachable — she just didn't want the drama it entailed tonight. She was still sporting several bruises, and underneath her foundation and the lowlights in the club, her face was still very much cut and swollen.

Stripper guy left, and Courtney found herself watching the groups on the dance floor, wishing she could have one more night out with the twins. Drew had never partied as often or as hard as her and Mel, but when she'd gone with them, it'd always been a blast. The last time they'd had a girls' night out, Cadence had been two months old, and Drew's breasts had started leaking milk on the dance floor. Drew had been mortified at the time, but now, looking back on it, Courtney thought it was hilarious.

"Woooo! I love this song!" Drew squealed, bursting into giggles and giving her ass a shake under the fog lights in the club. She was drunk, and it was such a rare occurrence that I made it my mission over the last couple of hours to record her a few times. The last time my bestie was drunk was … damn, sometime when she'd been battling her bulimia. And that had been the furthest possible from a happy, partying-with-the-girls drunk.

I lift my go-to club drink to my lips, and the Smirnoff drips down my chin when Mel knocks my elbow from the other side. "I didn't think baby girl would actually come out with us!" Mel admits, her hand covering the side of her mouth like she's telling me a secret, but even with her in heels I still have a few inches on her; I'd have had to lower my head if she was whispering, so my guess is she's too drunk to notice.

"It's nice being out with just my girls!" I exclaim, wrapping my arms around their shoulders and pulling them into me. We dance to the heavy bass of yet another favourite pop singer of Drew's, and I'm all too glad we left our significant others at home. Don't get me wrong, Natalie is fucking incredible in almost every way, but I still feel guarded as hell when she and Drew are in the same space. Natalie's been pissed off enough for a lifetime when it comes to my inconvenient feelings.

Drew's hand grazes my lower back, and even with the handful of drinks I've had, her touch is a hot caress to my soul. Even though our kiss weirded me out, and although I swore my crush on her had burned out, her standing in kissing distance fucks my head up. I pull my arm off the twins' shoulders and step back for a breather. It's there I notice the front of Drew's top has two large wet spots, one over each breast, and then a thin trail of whatever it is down her front. She's wearing a light-coloured halter-top, so it makes it even more noticeable.

I lean into her. "I think you might be uh ... leaking?" I say and wonder how out of it she is that she didn't notice her shirt is soaked. Drew has never been a big drinker, and even tonight she's had no more than three and she's toast.

When Drew stares back in confusion, I casually gesture to her chest, hoping nobody in the crowd noticed. Her face drops down to take in the situation, and a moment later, she's staring at me with huge saucers for eyes. "Oh nooo! That's never happened before!" Her lips make a perfect 'O,' and I have to stifle a laugh. It should be illegal to be so damn cute.

I grab Mel's hand and pry her away from the hot guy grinding against her; I wanted to take Drew to the restroom to get washed up, and I'd never hear the end of it if I left Mel on the dance floor. So I drag them away from the crowd and into the noisy washroom. As soon as Drew's inside, the state of her top begins to bother her. I catch her mortified expression in the mirror over the counter.

"I can't believe I didn't think to wear nursing pads," she wailed, blushing profusely as she stared at herself. Others are watching and a few even snickering, which makes me pissed. I stomp over to the nearest bitch and dump the rest of my Smirnoff over her head.

"That's for fucking laughing. Now get lost before the next thing that touches you is my fucking fist." They scatter like bees. I move to take over the part of the counter they'd been lounging on and notice Melanie giving me a doubtful look. "What?"

I tear paper towel out of the holder before turning to help dry up some of the breast milk. "You need to be careful talking to people like that, Court. You're sort of a VIP now around Van."

"Thanks." Drew takes the towels from me to pat down her breasts. It doesn't seem to be working all that well, and then she tucks the remainder of the paper towel in folded up wads inside her bra. Melanie announces she needs to pee and disappears into one of the stalls.

"You lied," Drew says, still sounding very tipsy. I pull my eyes from her chest to see her knowingly studying me. "Kris was right; you still have feelings for me."

Shit, now I'm blushing — also kicking myself for getting caught. What is going on with me? When I came back home, I was sure I was over Drew, but the more I spend time with her, the more that same annoying longing screws with my heart. "The alcohol's talking," I joke uneasily. "You're seeing things that aren't there."

"I thought you were gonna be open with me from now on?"

"Baby girl … no offense, but what's the point? It won't change what is," I murmur, and with the club music vibrating the walls of the bathroom, chances are she doesn't even hear me. I turn to grab a bit more paper towel from the dispenser.

Then her hand is on my face, her soft palm cupping my cheek that was still bruised from my sparring session with Natalie. She turns me in to her, resting her forehead against mine. She smells like beer. "I love you so much, Courtney Ann Cairns. And if I was into women, then I would only want you. You're my person, you know? Like Meredith and Cristina off Grey's. You're strong and smart, and such a babe. If I was into women, I'd wanna have sex with you all the time!"

I'm laughing by the time she's finished. Drew is reserved by nature, so hearing her shout out her if-only fantasy was fucking adorable. Melanie listening in just tops the scene, and when she exits the stall, she is staring at her sister in astonishment. She throws her head back and laughs. "How come we can't ever get Drew's drunk confessions on camera?"

I pull out my phone, waving it in her direction. "No confession, but lots of intoxicated footage."

Courtney gave herself a mental shake, cursing under her breath for falling victim to her bittersweet memories for even a second. There was a valid reason she kept her life before Drew's death under lock and key — it hurt too damn much to think about. She glanced down to her empty martini glass, wondering when she'd finished it. She signalled the bartender to pour her another. She was checking the time to see if it was too early yet to leave when Lou and Maxine nestled up beside her.

"C'mon, Corey, off that stool now," Max said, taking Courtney by the arm and briskly leading her away from the bar.

"It's time we found you a woman," Lou added, and Courtney noticed neither one gave her an explanation of where they'd been for the past forty minutes.

"I don't want a woman. Too much drama." But she let them lead her onto the dance floor anyway, and before she knew it, she was jamming to an ear-splitting techno beat. A handful of ladies flanked her, trying to steer her away from her friends, but she deflected every one of them. She couldn't describe it, but making out or having sex with someone at a club had lost its appeal. Her eyes were opened now; she'd had a sample of a real relationship where she connected to someone other than with their bodies. Sure, it'd left her gutted and seeping with emotional wounds, but it'd also left her full of longing for what had been.

When they left the club, they took a taxi back to Courtney's apartment. Why her place and not theirs she didn't know, but she didn't give a shit either way when they pulled out a bag of weed and a small pipe. Fuck, yes. She was past due for a flat-out, high-as-hell giggle fest where she didn't feel immediately guilty afterward.

"When's your next fight?" Max asked her lazily a while later. They were lounging on Courtney's sole sofa, and Max had her ankles crossed over the coffee table in the center like she lived there.

Courtney took the pipe carefully in one hand and lit the bowl of weed as she inhaled. She was grateful for the rapid mind-numbing, especially after reminiscing about Drew. "This coming Friday. I work till eight, then I've gotta jet. Won't know the location until about an hour before."

"And you don't know who you're fighting yet?" This came from Lou, who was curled into Max's body with a beer in her hand. They'd slipped into the bar downstairs to buy a case before they'd headed up to Courtney's place. She was currently sipping a glass of Merlot in between hits of weed.

"Nope, but likely one of the ones I fought before. There aren't many of us." She nestled into the sofa, crossing her legs and leaning her head against the back cushion. The weed was working its magic. She was floating now, all the stress in her life sifting up and away like fall leaves on a windy day. Fuck, she felt amazing. She couldn't recall what had had her so irritated earlier that night, and the low-decimal buzzing in her ears distracted her from their conversation. Kris's face popped in to her muddled thoughts, and then the bittersweet memory of getting high with him the Christmas before. A lot had gone on that day at Kris and Drew's apartment. Drew had been fighting with her mom around that time, so she'd decided to have a turkey dinner instead of going to her grandmother's with the family. Then she'd had a breakdown during dessert because the pie hadn't turned out great, and then Courtney had kissed Drew. To say it was an afternoon full of upheaval was an understatement. Kris's disappointed face soaked into her mind until his distrustful eyes were all she saw. She'd betrayed him that day, and yet he'd found it in him later to forgive her. For the relatively short time they'd known one another, they'd overcome their fair share of hurdles together.

"You fallin' asleep over there, Corey?"

Courtney cracked an eye open, a lazy grin forming. Her gaze landed on her ceiling, and for a moment she watched the overhead fan slowly spin. What had she been thinking about? "Shit, I'm baked. You guys wanna order pizza?"

DOBIE'S WIELDING HIS HUNTING knife in front of me, the long blade already glimmering with a thick coat of blood. The burning coming from my chest has me dropping my face down to see the gaping wound spilling my blood to the ground. A battle cry tears through me, and I trudge forward in full determination to end this fool. Except when my arms don't give behind me, I'm left puzzled and craning my neck to see what's holding me back. I've got myself in an adrenaline lock with Kris, and by the way our arms are tangled, the predicament was my idea. The truth dawns on me.

He's holding Cadence.

I must protect them at all costs.

"You fucking traitor, I'll kill you!" Dobie shouts, now swinging his blade out to stab Kris. He slashes him in the face before I'm able to kick him off once more.

Trepidation washes through me, and just like a movie I'd watched a thousand times, I have a sick feeling I know what's happing next.

But nothing at all could prepare me for it.

Dobie's hunting knife plunges into my stomach. I don't have time to process the pain because the blade's ripped out, and then he's stabbing me again and again. The blinding fire in my side is crippling, and I know he hit my lung.

I'm weakening.

It's taking everything left in me to keep my arms wrapped around Kris's. He's pulling, trying to wrench free of my hold, but I have to hold on. I just need to hold the fuck on.

The blade sinks into my flesh once more, and I feel my soul disperse as the weapon twists around my sternum. The startled breaths leaving my lips are precious last-minute gasps of life.

And then I'm falling...

Courtney woke with a dying scream still on her lips. She was soaked in sweat and shaking like she'd seen a ghost; she supposed she had, in a way. Living out one of Drew's last moments in the dream world had been fucking trippy. It was like she'd been Drew, seeing through her eyes, yet at the same time she'd still been Courtney. Hadn't she?

"Hell's bells, what's wrong with me?" she muttered, shoving a caked strand of hair off her cheek. The sheets on her pullout were damp from perspiration rolling off her bare skin, and her curls were matted to her scalp. Just how long had she been inside the nightmare?

Her throat felt raw as she pulled herself to a sitting position. Her fingers shook as she reached for the glass of water on the end table, so much that the liquid splashed out onto her hand. She took greedy gulps, washing down the ache the screaming had caused; washing down any remnants of the black-and-white images of Dobie stabbing her to death.

Fuck him. Fuck that psycho and his fetish for knives. He would get what was coming to him, if he hadn't already. She was certain there'd be tons of his enemies in prison, eagerly waiting for the moment to shank him in the shower or when he was sleeping. She'd do it herself if given the chance.

Fumbling for her glasses, she put them on over unfocused eyes. She felt out of it from the nightmare. She slid out of bed, letting the tangled sheets pool at her ankles, and walked naked to her bathroom. Upon a quick inspection of her body in the mirror, she saw the place she'd split her knuckles in the last fight had partially reopened. She must have struck it on the nightstand while she'd been battling Dobie in her dream state. Blood had smeared and dried on her chest and along her throat; it struck her as odd that her sweat hadn't washed it away.

She started the shower, making sure the temperature was melting-the-bones hot before she climbed in under the spray. The water burned her scalp before scorching her back — the abrasive remedy was exactly what she needed in that moment. Grabbing a facecloth from the shelf above the toilet, she ran the material under the hot spray before squirting on some bodywash. As she washed her arms and torso, a random image of washing Natalie popped into her high-strung awareness.

"You make me feel so beautiful, Court. Beautiful and wanted. Mmm ... I love you."

Courtney's eyes closed. She could practically feel Natalie's soft skin under her hands, her tantalizing curves and the two moles on her back. She'd always smelt so pretty and fresh, like flowers after a spring rain.

"I can't wait to marry you."

It was too bad they'd never gotten that far. Courtney had seen to it by doing the most cowardly thing possible to end their engagement. She sighed, reaching for the shaving cream and lathering a leg before picking up the razor. When she was scrubbed clean and shaved, she turned off the taps and reached for a towel. Once she was dried off and dressed in a simple athletic top and cargo pants with her hair pulled into a ponytail, she sat down to put on her makeup.

She'd been applying makeup since she was a tween, and although Kris always insisted she didn't need any, she felt naked and exposed without it. She pulled her makeup bag from the vanity cupboard, sifting through the contents until she found her primer. When she'd rubbed that into her face, she selected her two cases of eyeshadow from the bag. Most people she knew made this the second-last step, but she found it a time-saver in case some dropped on her face as she was putting it on. Shutting one eye at a time, she applied a lighter-tint eyeshadow first on the upper part of her lid right under her eyebrow, and then a bolder shade of brown on the bottom part of her lid. When she was satisfied with how it looked, she retrieved the foundation and illuminator. They helped transform her pale redhead features into a woman guys and girls alike tripped over each other to get to. She gently rubbed them in with her makeup brush. The concealer she applied next helped better disguise the evidence of her fighting.

She returned to her eyes, adding a thin layer of eyeliner and mascara to really make her eyes pop. Then she spread on a bronzer to give her face a bit of glow before using a setting spray. She'd run out of the spray and was certain that was why her makeup ran the other night at work. The last step was her lipliner and lipstick, and she spread the products onto her lips one at a time. She puckered them in the mirror, turning her face side to side to check out her work. Not too shabby.

Out in the kitchen, she set about boiling water for coffee and pulling out the eggs and bacon, determined as hell she wouldn't burn them again. She cracked the eggs into a bowl, grimacing when she had to dig out numerous bits of shell. She'd been raised in a house with employed staff who cooked and cleaned for her, so learning to manage these things on her own was an adjustment. She'd discovered over the last year that she had absolutely zero knack for cooking and doubted it would ever change. She tried, though, desperate to feel the excitement and passion Drew used to when it came to creating a meal. Courtney had spent a lot of her time at the Matheson house over the years just watching Drew zoom around the kitchen.

When the food was cooking on the stove, she poured the hot water onto the fresh coffee grounds in her French press. She was cutting up grapefruit when the smoke detector went off. "Shit," she grumbled, turning back to the stove. Sure enough, she'd turn on the wrong burner and was now melting the spatula she'd placed there. She snatched it off the hot burner, still cursing.

"At least I have the eggs and toast," she conceded before remembering she hadn't put the bread in the toaster. Still grumbling, she scraped the sloppy-looking eggs onto a plate with her grapefruit and coffee. She sat down to eat but suddenly didn't feel all that hungry. She wouldn't serve these eggs to her worst enemy, let alone herself. On second thought ... she'd totally serve them to Dobie, alongside a poisonous apple and rat bait.

"Fuck this," she decided, scraping her chair back and grabbing her apartment keys off the counter. She wasn't desperate enough to eat the shit on her plate. Life was too short.

She was taking herself out for breakfast.

Chapter 4

Location Undisclosed, January 18

COURTNEY LOOKED ON THROUGH the makeshift fence separating the fighters in the "ring" from the spectators. The match happening now was between two men who both appeared tough and very skilled in their chosen styles of martial arts. It looked like Muay Thai, which was essentially a much more advanced version of kickboxing. The spectators around her were shouting encouragement to the fighters — many of them with face coverings to obscure their features in case someone was filming. Courtney paid attention to none of that, and she felt the noise fade away as she focused on the men in the ring.

She was up next.

She reached up to make sure her long curls were still secure in the tight bun and then moved her head from side to side, stretching her neck and shrugging several times to loosen any kinked muscles. It was hard to believe two years ago she'd never considered kickboxing as a tool to let off steam, and now look at her. It was crazy, but being here made sense to Courtney. She was hurting so deep inside that she didn't think she'd truly smiled since the day of the marathon. It was the last day she remembered being happy. Crazy or not, she felt like she belonged with the fighters around her. They were all there for one reason or another — and less often than one might think was it for the money or recognition.

"He's got him. He's got him in the bag!" the guy behind her exclaimed in an excited crow as the larger fighter successfully pinned the smaller one down on the ground. The little guy repeatedly tried and failed to break loose of the wrestling lock, to no avail.

Others around her agreed, all hoping or at least expecting the larger fighter to win. Courtney chose not to weigh in on the conversation either way; having said that, a fight wasn't over till it was over, so she was half hoping the little guy wiggled out of that grip somehow.

A few minutes later, she was disappointed as the smaller guy tapped out of the fight. She raised her eyebrow, watching as they shook hands before they left the ring. They both were in rough shape; both looked like they did what they came there to do. Even if you lost in these underground fight clubs, the amount of respect people gave the loser was impressive. Courtney had never seen anything like it.

Her Spidey sense started going berserk again as she felt the now familiar tingling sensation racing down her spine. She shivered, but it had nothing to do with the weather. She casually glanced around her, immediately spotting a well-built guy staring at her from several feet away. His face was obscured, and he had a toque on so she couldn't see his hair, but somehow she knew it was the creep who'd been following her.

She narrowed her eyes, refusing to feel threatened by a piece of shit like him. What the fuck was he about, anyway? She'd been racking her head for days trying to imagine why someone would be following her. She'd only come up with the obvious — she'd been identified from her father's company — but even so, what would they even want with her? Had her father done a shady business deal, and now they were looking at getting even?

What if it had nothing to do with that at all? Hell, maybe her fighting had gained interest from the wrong people, and now they were keeping tabs on her. Nothing made fucking sense, and she was sick of being tailed.

Shouldering her bag, she was heading his way when she heard her name on the PA, temporarily distracting her from her mission, and she glanced to the ring.

"Next match — Corey against Kiki!" the ref called out from the center of the ring.

"Go get her, Corey!" the guy beside her hollered in triumph.

Fuck, now where did he go? Courtney thought, glancing around for the mysterious guy and coming up empty. The crowd was large enough that he blended in and disappeared from her line of vision seamlessly, and she huffed a frustrated sigh.

She took a deep breath, shaking her shoulders again as she gave up for the time being and refocused her thoughts on her fight. That fucker could wait; her schedule was already full for ass-kicking tonight.

Nervous anticipation rumbled through Courtney as she made her way to the center and wondered who this Kiki was. She must have been new, since Courtney was sure she'd fought everyone there was. Spectators and fighters alike cleared a narrow path for her, and when she reached the makeshift barrier, she squeezed through the opening. The location of the club was ever changing, since they were banned from just about everywhere. Tonight's scenery backdrop was the top floor of a parkade, but every time was different. The last fight she'd been in was inside an old warehouse.

She shrugged out of her zippered hoodie, exposing her sports bra over her blue athletic pants. She dropped the hoodie and her duffel bag in the corner out of the way and tried not to think about the creep in the crowd likely watching. Her opponent came into the space behind her, and when Courtney faced her, she did a shocked double-take. What the fuck else was tonight going to throw at her?

Kiki looked just like Natalie, unassuming and casually pretty, with straight black hair pulled back and gorgeous brown eyes. She seemed leaner than Natalie, maybe, and she didn't appear to have a dimple in her chin, but fuck the jawline, the shape of her eyes and how the locks of hair curled at the end of her ponytail...

Courtney's pulse was racing so fast that it and the pounding in her head were all she could feel and hear as she met Kiki/Natalie in the middle of the ring. No longer giving a shit about the enigmatic guy with his eyes on her, she couldn't stop staring wide-eyed at the girl within arm's reach; she felt sucker-punched before the match even started.

The ref must have said his piece, because he left them, and then Kiki/Natalie broke away from Courtney. Courtney stood there dumbly, watching as the other girl circled her. She knew she should be trying to get a punch in or something but — "Natalie?" she asked, just to be sure she wasn't wrong. Except Natalie wouldn't travel all the way to the states just to bring Courtney home. Only Drew would have done something so loving and selfless.

The fist connecting with her gaping mouth told her all she needed to know; unfortunately, it didn't help her bounce out of her stunned stupor. She was off her game, sloppy with her return attacks. Courtney's ex was on her mind now, guilt tearing at her as she remembered how she'd just disappeared early the morning after Drew's funeral. Natalie had still been in bed, not realizing her lover had packed a bag just to vanish out of her life. Things had been going so well with them too; they'd finally reached a blissful moment in their relationship without all the drama circling Drew and Courtney's affections for her BFF. They'd been happy; hell, before Drew had been stabbed, Courtney and Natalie had even gotten reengaged.

Another blow came swiftly, this time a strong kick to her ribs, making Courtney gasp as pain laced through her. "What the fuck are you doing? Fight me!"

Courtney shook out of her daze, briefly hearing the spectators shouting similar phrases. She dodged the next punch Kiki/Natalie threw at her, instead grabbing her shoulder and ramming her knee into her stomach. It wasn't a kickboxing move, but anything went in these fights. Feeling like she finally got the upper hand, Courtney pivoted, about to swing into her roundhouse kick and overconfident as hell she'd knock her opponent out. She didn't anticipate what came next.

The attack came out of nowhere, momentarily lifting her right off the ground. Courtney's eyes widened in surprise, and she realized the superpowered Kiki/Natalie had her arms squeezed around her. She cried out as her shoulder connected with the asphalt, incredible pain exploding all over her body.

Courtney was doing everything possible not to bawl like a baby, and the crazy MMA fighter got in a handful more punches before she found the strength to call the match. It killed her to do it, but she tapped Kiki's thigh with the arm that was still functional. When she was released, it was in just enough time to spit out her mouthpiece and throw up. The ref bent down to see if she was okay, but she declined his help. Her opponent came over to shake her hand, but Courtney ignored her effort, instead hobbling to her feet on a pair of uncertain legs. She knew it was poor sportsmanship not to shake, but tears were stinging the backs of her eyelids, and all Courtney wanted to do was grab her shit and go home. Blood was spattered on her bag from her lip, and she carefully positioned it over her good left shoulder. Her right arm hung frozen in midair, as if it was already in a sling, completely out of alignment with her dislocated shoulder.

The crowd opened a path for her again, this time falling into hushed silence as she went past. It was so quiet, she could hear her uneven breaths in the night air, and she was so cold now, her lips chattered as she made her way down to the street. Nausea made her dizzy, and she hurled once more before she got to her apartment above the bar. Tears rolled down her cheeks as she gazed into the bathroom mirror, not even caring about the cuts on her face or her split lip. She should have gone to the hospital. Her shoulder socket stuck out like an abomination, making her entire arm off-kilter. Perspiration soaked her forehead, and she cringed at the idea of knocking it back into place herself. With a low moan, she snatched the bottle of Advil off the back of the toilet, struggling to hold it in her hand with the bad shoulder so she could open it.

"Stupid fucking push tabs," Courtney groaned, finally giving up and biffing the bottle into the bathtub.

Pain had her trembling as she made her way into the kitchen. She pulled down her bottle of vodka, twisting off the cap with her teeth and not caring about the blood her mouth left in its wake. She chugged the bitter liquid down in thirsty gulps and prayed it would take the edge off what she was about to do.

She grabbed a clean towel, sloppily rolling it up so she could bite it. She'd seen a dislocated shoulder being popped back into place years ago in high school, so she was only going on vague memory. Taking several more chugs of the liquor, she was already feeling the effects as she picked up the rolled towel and placed it between her teeth. Then she faced the bathroom door frame.

This would be a whole lot easier with another person.

"Fuck it," she decided, taking a deep breath before charging into the edge of the door frame. Her shoulder made contact all right, and Courtney screamed as all it did was bring the pain level up several notches. She was so fucking nauseated now, the entire room was spinning. She knew at once she was about to pass out.

She did, not even having the chance to make it to the sofa first.

COURTNEY REGAINED CONSCIOUSNESS VERY slowly, immediately aware something soft rested under her weight. It certainly raised alarms, because she was positive she'd passed out on the floor near the bathroom. She licked her dry lips, stopping when she came across the abrasive stitching embedded into her bottom lip.

"What the—" she muttered, her eyes flying open to dart around. The late morning light cascading through the open windows worsened the stabbing behind her eyes, and she winced. Between the headache and her nausea, she had the symptoms of a hangover, but she didn't remember drinking enough to warrant such an effect.

What the hell was going on?

She was lying on the sofa, for god's sake, her arm in a sling for real this time. Her shoulder wasn't bothering her as much, and if she didn't know any better, she'd have thought she'd taken herself to the hospital. Glancing to the coffee table next to the sofa she was somehow on, she noticed her two cell phones and house keys on one side and a small garbage can filled with bloodied gauze on the other.

Someone had tended to her last night.

Sudden panic had her flying up from the sofa, which she instantly regretted doing as every part of her rebelled. Half out of it, her breaths were coming out short and choppy as she scanned her apartment for danger. No sign of anyone there, nothing out of place except for the items neatly arranged on her coffee table. And her clothes, she slowly noted; her socks and sweater had been folded and placed on the edge of the sofa.

Someone had been *in* her apartment, likely *drugged* her, and then nursed her back to health. By the stitches in her lip and her reset shoulder, she'd guess some legitimate mending had gone down.

Courtney's first thought was mama Jen, since Drew's mother was an ER doctor, or at least she had been before receiving guardianship over Cadence. But it didn't make sense that Jennifer would track Courtney down and then disappear again. Or maybe she'd just stepped out?

Courtney shook her head, disagreeing with such logic. She stood up, heading to the long mirror hanging on the apartment door. Her arm rested comfortably in the sling, and the stitches in her lip could certainly have been done by a doctor. The little cuts on her cheeks were still noticeable, but nothing was bleeding. All in all, she still looked worse for wear but was a hell of a lot more put together than last night.

She went to the sink for a drink, thinking about the man who'd been watching her at the fight and the other instances of being tailed. Could it have been him in here taking care of her? He was an unknown and clearly someone with an ulterior motive. Her stomach twisted as another thought entered her fuzzy brain.

Hell's bells, he could legitimately be a stalker. Didn't stalkers show concern and affection before escalating into killing their victim?

This was bad. This was really bad. Some creep pursuing her was the most plausible answer to this insane situation, and fuck him if he thought she'd stick around to watch him escalate. She broke out in a cold sweat at the thought of the creeper touching her when she was unaware. Considering she had no recollection of being someone's patient, and she'd only had a handful of swigs of the vodka, she was certain she'd been drugged. Being that vulnerable had her in a severe panic.

She was leaving, today. It was clear she'd outstayed her welcome in New York. But where could she go? Her passport would expire soon enough, so continuing in the States was a no-go, but that was a good thing, right? Surely Mr. Big, Strong, and Stalkerish wouldn't tail her out of country? She wasn't that fucking interesting.

Her body had been through the ringer, and so she pulled her extra duffel from the closet slower than she'd like. Her bruised ribs were making her breath wonky as she emptied out the lone dresser in the apartment. She wouldn't be able to take all her stuff with her this time, since she'd foolishly gotten comfortable in this city and had bought extra clothes to work in the bar. She was going to miss it there, she decided. Over the last several months, she'd gotten used to the banter between the patrons and staff, and it seemed almost familial most days. Everyone there had a past, and no one asked questions. You were judged by your character now, not who you might've been — which fit Courtney perfectly; in her mind, she'd have had a lot to be judged on for past mistakes. Every choice she did or didn't make — it all landed her here, in this moment, with her arm in a sling and a stalker only god knows where.

"Just what you deserve, isn't it, *Red*?" Courtney sarcastically muttered, slamming her bag down again. For not doing more to save Drew, she deserved this and a hell of a lot more.

Chapter 5

Moncton Bus Depot, January 20

I'M SCREAMING IN AGONY as I greet the fear in Drew's eyes. Dobie shoves her away, like killing her is just a fucking job that needs doing. I can't get to her fast enough, and she's falling, falling in slow motion to the ground.

Dobie's laughter is everywhere, drowning out the frantic crowd, drowning out my own sobs. He's tried to kill the most beautiful person, and all he can do is laugh.

"Fucking psycho," I snap, and as I rush past him being pinned down by security, I kick him in the face. If I had the time, I'd see how he likes the pain of the blade while I cut out his cold, dead heart.

I fall to my knees in front of Drew, trying so hard to stop the bleeding. I can hear her shallow breaths; or is that me? I'm terrified. The fear and anger cast a heavy veil around us, around me, threatening to overtake me as true as death is at baby girl's doorstep.

"You guys ... love me?"

I soak up Drew's face, pretending I'm seeing her for the first time instead of the last. Her soft skin is now ashen as she bleeds out, her adorable ears that she's always disliked, the way her nose turns up just so. Her gentle, storm-cloud-grey eyes hold mine. Do I love her? Fuck, when have I not? I've held a torch for this girl half of my life, but she doesn't know the full extent of my feelings.

She doesn't know that she's been it for me since that summer we played spin the bottle. Now she might never know, like really know, how deep and how real my feelings are.

"You know we love you. More than anyone," I choke out, but her eyes are closing. Was I too late; did she not hear? I spent priceless moments thinking of what I'd say, and what if she never hears it?

Drew coughs, and in horror I watch as blood oozes out between her beautiful lips. Then she's mouthing something, but I can't hear her. I glance at Kris, and a startled cry escapes me; Kris has turned into Drew, and she's staring at me.

"Take care of them, Courtney. Love them ... like you love me."

The coolness of tears on her cheeks woke Courtney from her desolate dreams. Before she even opened her eyes, she was blindly swiping them away and grimaced at the tenderness under her lashes from the beating Kiki had given her. The ache in her chest was fresh, and it felt an awful lot like she'd reopened an old internal wound yet again. "Fuck, when will they stop?" she muttered and immediately fumbled with the zipper pocket on her jacket. She retrieved her old phone, breathing a ragged sigh as she soaked up Drew's face on the display screen. Seeing the healthy glow in her skin and her irresistible lips free of blood calmed Courtney, but she knew it was a lie; mere short-lived relief. She licked her own lips, moistening the chafing stitches embedded on the bottom.

Still sniffling, she glanced around, and it took a second to remember where she'd fallen asleep. She'd been halfway to New Brunswick before she realized she'd bought the wrong ticket. She'd meant to head farther west, but panicked Courtney must have subconsciously been looking for comfort. From whom, she wasn't entirely sure, but she knew Natalie's parents lived about an hour away. She couldn't have been thinking straight, because there was no way in hell she'd ever land on their doorstep looking for help or a hug. After what she did to Natalie, Frank and Sally would probably rather choke her than offer compassion.

She checked the time on her watch and cursed when she realized she'd miss her bus if she didn't haul ass. So she wiped her eyes again with her good arm and scrambled awkwardly to her feet to grab her bags. She still needed to pee and buy snacks at the vending machine.

Courtney's heart stuttered as she took in the lone duffel bag she'd been sleeping on, her backpack nowhere to be found. She'd swear on her favourite San Francisco stilettos that she'd been holding on to the straps when she'd fallen asleep. "Calm down, calm down; don't fucking panic." She took a deep breath, slowly turning in a full circle in hopes the lost bag would reveal itself. She glanced under the uncomfortable chair she'd sat on before she'd moved to the floor to sleep. No backpack — and what was worse than no fucking backpack? She'd stuffed her purse inside it with all her cash and ID.

"Is there something I can help you find, dear?"

Courtney froze in her pointless search, straightening up to find the same older lady that had sold her a ticket hours ago. And once again she was looking at Courtney with grave sympathy. She probably thought Courtney had been beaten up by a boyfriend. "My backpack is gone; a blue grey Adidas one with pink zipper ties. I had my purse inside." She frowned, despising the slight tremble in her voice.

"Oh no, that's awful! Did you check the bathroom or ask any of the bus drivers? Maybe you left it somewhere."

"You think four hours ago I wouldn't have noticed if I had two bags or one with me?" Courtney demanded. She threw her good hand up in exasperation, and when it landed hard against her side, it jarred her recovering shoulder. A sick sensation rolled through her, and she briefly closed her eyes. "Never mind. Can you check the security feed? Maybe you can track down whoever stole it. I'm gonna miss the bus at this rate."

It was a damn good thing she wasn't in a rush. The only thing, er, person, she'd been running from was still in New York. She was confident about that. She hadn't seen anyone even closely resembling her stalker in two days. All she wanted to do now was sink down in a hot bubble bath with a glass of

Merlot and figure out what her next step would be. Fighting was obvious — well, as soon as she was healed — but she also needed shelter.

"This must be so frustrating for you to go through, dear. Why don't you follow me, and I'll see if we can't resolve this, okay? I'm sure Danny can check the cameras for you."

"Thank you."

"No problem, dear. I'm Loraine, by the way."

"Corey." She said the name without thinking; after a year of saying or hearing it, she'd grown accustomed to her alter ego. Courtney followed silently behind the older woman, appreciating her East Coast warmth. It made her miss Natalie something awful, though, and as she stood behind the security guy, watching for whoever stole her shit to show his face, she couldn't stop thinking about her ex. They'd taken a trip together to New Brunswick just over a year ago. Natalie had taken her home to meet her parents, her family, and the town where she'd grown up. Courtney had adored the simple beauty of the places Natalie had taken her. It was actually one of the rare times in Courtney's life when she'd been truly happy. She'd felt free here, away from the pressures of her family's business, away from her unrequited love for Drew. She'd proposed to Natalie on the walking trails at Hopewell Rocks, a hundred percent convinced everything would work out in the end.

What a fucking joke that had been.

"...knew exactly where the cameras were," Danny was saying. Courtney shook herself from her daze, aware he was staring up at her from his chair. His sympathetic face had her grinding her molars down. "I'm sorry, miss. I haven't a clue how to track this guy down. We can call the police and file a report. Is there anyone you can call for a ride, somewhere safe that you can go?"

"Somewhere safe ... what? No, of course not," Courtney snapped before she had time to reel herself in. She scowled, certain her eyes were blazing. "If I had someone to come get me, I wouldn't be here sleeping and getting my fucking shit stolen. And now I've missed the bus, but it's no matter, now right? My ticket was in that bag."

She was fuming; she felt like her head would pop off any minute. *Breathe, Courtney, fucking breathe, girl. It's not his fault.* "I'm sorry," she muttered, picking up her duffel bag and leaving the room before she said something else rude.

Loraine met her in the hallway with a coupon for the next bus. Courtney started to reach for it until Loraine mentioned the next one wasn't coming for another two days. "Are you kidding me right now?"

She had the worst damn luck! What was she going to do now? She had funds tied into her bank accounts, but as soon as she touched it, her father would figure out where she was. What was the point in falling off-grid if she went to her bank account anytime she needed? No, she needed to figure this out for herself. She wasn't the same Courtney Cairns she'd been in B.C.; she no longer had any interest in throwing money at every problem.

"Dear, are you all right? I'd have to be blind not to notice ... you know. Are you in trouble?" she heard Loraine asking in the distance. "You're welcome to stay with me for the night until you figure something out."

Courtney shook her head, only vaguely listening to her, but knew enough to decline the invitation. "No, no thanks. I need to ... I just need to take a walk." Without another word, she left the depot. She felt numb despite the cold February temperatures, and for quite a while she strolled aimlessly around downtown Moncton. It didn't make sense that she'd say no to a warm bed for a night. She just knew she didn't want her defective personality around such a sweet lady as Loraine. What she *wanted* to do was track down the fucker who'd stolen from her and cut off all his fingers. Was that a normal response to something like this? Or was she getting colder inside, *deader*, like Dobie in her nightmare?

She should just be thankful her cell phone had been in her jacket and the chargers in her duffel bag. She still had enough clothes to get by — a few sets plus her workout sneakers. And another set of hat and gloves in case these got lost.

She found herself shivering in front of a house-style restaurant and still needing badly to pee. Her shoulders were stiff from carrying the weight of her duffel bag on one side, and her dislocated arm was aching inside the sling. It had to be the worst damn time to travel, not that her stalker had given her much choice in the matter. If it'd been up to her, she'd still be sleeping in her New York apartment.

Courtney climbed the stairs and pushed open the door to the restaurant, and the sudden onslaught of heat on her face was remarkable. She paused there for a moment, letting her eyes close as the warmth cascaded over her.

"Looks like you could use a hot cup of something," a woman said to her with a smile as she and her husband walked past to the door.

"That's an understatement," Courtney murmured after they'd left. She pulled her toque and mittens off, scanning the handful of patrons in the restaurant as she located the restroom.

"Morning. Take a seat wherever," a waitress greeted her as she headed to a table with a tray of food.

"Thank you," Courtney replied, but instead of sitting, she beelined it for the washroom. It'd been a long while since she'd last peed, and she was praying she didn't piss herself as she scrambled to take her coat off and undo her pants in the stall. Fucking Kiki with her world-class tackle, and fucking Courtney for being distracted during the fight in the first damn place.

She felt like crying as she rested her head against the wall of the stall. She was just so tired, both mentally and physically, and cold all the time. She couldn't remember a time in her previous life when she'd felt winter right to her frickin' bones. She wouldn't be surprised if she came out of this with arthritis or some other joint-depleting condition the cold thrived on tormenting.

"You've *got* to be fucking kidding me," she said for the second time that morning as she noticed she'd started her period. What gave, really?

She bent over in search of supplies inside her duffel, and when she only found two remaining tampons, tears of frustration glimmered in her eyes. She'd meant to pick more up when she'd landed somewhere. She hadn't anticipated having her purse stolen and being down to her last few dollars. "Suck it up, Corey," Courtney muttered as she wiped and inserted the tampon. "You're stronger than this, so get it the fuck together."

She was washing her hands when she remembered her toiletry bag was in her duffel. "Thank you," she whispered to the ceiling, unsure these days of who she was thanking but certain Drew was watching out for her. If her bestie had been watching during the thievery of her backpack, she'd probably tried to guide the guy in the holy direction of returning it instead of kicking his ass. Courtney laughed at that image as she dug through her bag once more. She brushed her teeth before retrieving one of the face cloths she'd thought to pack and a bar of soap. Once she'd had a quick sponge bath, she strung her coat overtop the bag and left the bathroom. She spotted a vacant table in the back right away and ambled over to slide her heavy bag in first. She was feeling better a million times over after freshening up, but the optimism fled when she pulled out the sole remaining money zippered on the inside pocket of her coat. Her bubble slowly deflated as she set a single five-dollar bill on the table, a looney, and forty-five cents in change.

Not even enough to buy a decent meal.

She saw a different waitress coming toward her with a place setting, and she quickly gathered the cash to stuff into her thermal jeans.

"Morning. Can I get you something to drink to start you off?"

Courtney nodded, silently contemplating what she could buy. "A coffee, please, and I'll just have a muffin — blueberry or bran if you have it, with butter on the side."

"No problem." The woman turned away.

"Wait, sorry," Courtney said, realizing there wouldn't be enough protein in the muffin. She'd be starving before long without it. She cleared her throat, wondering what else she could buy. "How much is a side of eggs?"

"Two bucks plus tax."

Shit. She chewed her lip, and when she didn't reply, the waitress said she'd be back with the coffee. Courtney's face flushed, unable to believe she was this broke. Was this how Kris had felt for most of his life? Constantly having to decide what to buy and what he'd have to sacrifice to buy it? She used to get so exasperated watching him scour the menu for the cheapest meal available whenever they'd go for breakfast.

"Mommy, why did we sleep in the car? It was cold to sleep there."

Courtney glanced at the table across from hers, spotting a chubby-cheeked little boy, maybe three or four, sitting beside his baby sister, who was in a highchair. The little girl couldn't have been any more than a year old, way too young to be sleeping in a car during an eastern Canadian winter. What kind of mother would do that?

"AJ, whisper, honey, remember? And you didn't like sleeping there? I thought it would be fun for us to all be together, like a cozy campout. Do you remember when we slept in the tent this summer?"

"Here you go; have you decided what you'll have to eat?" the waitress asked Courtney, carefully pouring coffee into her mug. She pulled cream and sugar out of her apron to set beside her.

Courtney's cheeks flushed when she saw the mother quickly glance at her, as if she'd heard the prior conversation with the waitress. She feigned a smile, handing the waitress back her menu. "I'll just get the muffin. Thanks."

"Be right back." Wariness plagued the woman's demeanour, like she knew already Courtney's tip would be nonexistent.

She sipped her coffee and wondered what her next plan would be. She couldn't be sure, of course, but she had a strong feeling Moncton was lacking in underground fight clubs. She *needed* to get farther west, maybe even luck out and find a Workaway to bide her time. She'd had a handful around the country after she'd left B.C., doing anything from making beds to strawberry picking to baling hay. Better yet, if she could get work bartending again, it'd bring in enough income that she could start to save a little money again.

She was still mulling ideas over when the waitress brought her the muffin, as well as two boiled eggs. Courtney looked up at her in confusion.

"The bleeding heart in the kitchen took one look at you and insisted I get you some eggs. So here you go; hope you like 'em boiled."

"Thank you, really. I won't forget this," Courtney said, sounding every bit as grateful as she was, and a whole lot embarrassed. Was this how it felt to anyone ever receiving a handout? In the past, she'd been the one to endlessly give; although she'd known it felt good to give what she had, she never realized how hard it must've been for the person taking from her. She kept returning to Kris for some reason, maybe because he was the only one she knew and called a friend that had been through real-life hardships. He must have really loved Drew and wanted to get better to accept Courtney paying for his therapy for so long.

"Uh-huh. Enjoy your breakfast. Would you like more coffee?"

"Please." The waitress could have used an attitude adjustment, but Courtney kept that to herself as she slowly ate. The coffee was house special beans or something else equally weak and boring, but it was hot. She'd treat herself to a latte whenever she got back on her feet. It felt like forever since she'd eaten breakfast out, and she found herself longing for those past moments with Kris. They'd grab a bite to eat a couple times a week while Drew had been away for treatment, and even afterward, when Drew and Kris had had a place of their own, he'd still meet for breakfast once a week. He'd become a close friend over time, which was why it hurt Courtney so much that he'd been so fucking careless with Drew and Cadence's safety.

She kept her head down as she nibbled her muffin but could hear the table next to her speaking in hushed tones. By all appearances, they seemed to be down on their luck as well. The little boy's hair was shaggy and tangled, in desperate need of a cut, and the bags under his eyes was a sure sign he was lacking sleep. The mother looked worn out, and the extreme stress shadowing her face made it difficult to guess her age; it could have been anywhere between late twenties to late thirties. Her daughter looked to be in the best shape out of the three, well fed and clean, and Courtney questioned the reasons for it. Were they sacrificing their care for the little girl's? Or was it more suspicious to anyone watching if a baby was unclean and hungry, as opposed to a little boy?

"Is Daddy still mad? Is that why he's not having a campout with us?"

The hair on the back of Courtney's neck stood up at the boy, AJ's heartfelt whisper. Something was legit going on here, and she casually craned her ear closer to eavesdrop on the mother's response.

"No, baby. This campout is special, for just you, and Carley, and me. We'll do all sorts of fun things, just wait."

Courtney shook her head, deciding she didn't want to get involved in whatever was going on. She had enough shit on her plate as it was. She hurried to eat, eager now to get on the road. She didn't want to spend any more time than she had to in the province, and she figured if she could hitch a ride, it'd be faster than waiting for another bus. So, when she was all done, she reached into the side pocket of her duffel bag and retrieved her pocketknife. She'd bought it for protection when she'd started her journey on the road, and she'd quickly found out holding on to the small weapon made her feel a hell of a lot safer whenever she had to hitchhike. Thankfully, it'd never been needed, but mostly because she never hitchhiked at night and never got in a car with men.

When she was paying for her meal, she felt the need to explain to the not-so-friendly waitress that she'd had her bag stolen at the bus depot, hence the lack of funds. But when she was leaving, she couldn't help but question her current lack of confidence. Normally, if something less than ideal happened to her, she'd laugh it off and pretend it was her idea; or if someone was a bitch, she'd tell them off before she could even think about stopping herself. The only reason she could think of for this humiliating lady balls deflater was she'd been robbed and was now broke as fuck.

She squared her shoulders, staring straight ahead as she headed toward the highway and ignoring the occasional curious glances. So, she had a black eye and stitches in her lip. So, she was already cold, already tired, and her bag was hurting her other shoulder. Who the fuck cared? She didn't. She'd put herself in this position, and she was going to fight like hell to get herself out.

Chapter 6

SHE'D ONLY BEEN WALKING an hour at most when the first vehicle slowly pulled onto the shoulder of the highway, and Courtney sighed in relief. She'd been seriously doubting her ability to continue onward, but when she hurried to reach the truck rumbling toward her, she froze midstep.

"That's okay," she called to the heavy-set man behind the steering wheel. He looked friendly in a nonthreatening way, but so did a lot of rapists and serial killers. She politely waved him off, skirting her eyes back to the road and grateful the traffic was continuous. At least she'd have witnesses if Jekyll became Hyde.

"Are you sure? It's twenty-three below today; you must be freezing." His voice carried through the open window.

She was past freezing. She'd reached the warm and numb part, but there was no way in hell she'd get in the truck with him. Even with her self-defense skills, he'd have an advantage with his build. When she continued to walk away, the man got the hint and drove off. Courtney kept on, once again walking backward a ways with her thumb stuck out. Some nice woman would eventually pick her up, hopefully with a box of tampons and a picnic basket full of food and tea and wine.

"The fuck, Courtney? Are you looking for a ride or a date?" she muttered, wincing a little as her bag chafed her shoulder. She snickered, realization dawning on her that she spoke to herself way too much these days. She'd never been a loner, had always made a huge effort to surround herself with people. In fact, the thought of being on her own had terrified her. Not on a trip or to the movies alone, but truly alone, like she'd been for close to a year. No one to call and invite over when she was lonesome, no one to come watch her fights or go shopping with. She didn't have a partner to wake up beside, go to bed with, fight and make up ...

She wasn't paying attention when the next vehicle pulled over for her to get in. This time it was a grey four-door car with a couple guys around her age. A year ago, she would've taken either or both home from the bar, drunk as shit and not giving a fuck about anything.

"Hey, thanks for stopping, guys, but I'm good," Courtney said, and as they drove off, she was half applauding and half loathing her determination over her hitchhiking rules. She thought she'd freeze to death stranded on the highway when finally another car stopped for her. She'd decided after she'd sent the guys off that she'd get in the next vehicle no matter what; she was stubborn but not stupid.

Thankfully, she didn't have to make a complicated decision, because it was a woman behind the wheel. Courtney waved, so grateful she could cry, or maybe that was the exhaustion plaguing her. As she reached the passenger side door, she noted the sleeping children in the back seat.

"You look like you're dying a slow death out here. I'll give you a ride, so long as you don't mind the occasional crying kid."

Recognition dawned on her as she studied the woman and knew she had mouse-brown hair under her winter hat. "I saw you guys earlier, right? At the restaurant."

The woman nodded and then jerked her thumb toward the back of the car. "I'll pop the trunk; it'll be a tight squeeze, but your bag should fit."

"Thank you. God, thank you so much!"

"Nope, not God. Just Katie." One corner of her mouth tilted up in the beginnings of a smile. She suddenly looked younger, probably no more than thirty.

Courtney didn't know why, but she had a strong urge to tell Katie her real name. She was considering it as she pulled open the trunk. "Shit, you weren't lying," Courtney muttered, taking in the storage space jam-packed with their suitcases.

"Here, let me help." Katie appeared beside her so silently that Courtney jumped a little. The woman walked like a frickin' ghost! Katie frowned, watching her step back out of the way. "I figured you could use the help, since it looks like you only got one good arm."

"Yeah, thanks." Courtney swallowed, glancing over Katie's shoulder to see more cars zoom past. "My uh, I dislocated my shoulder. My arm isn't broke or anything."

"Okay." Katie nodded, closing the trunk once more.

"Where you headed?" she asked Courtney when they were on the road.

Courtney didn't take her bare hands off the car heater as she replied, "Toronto. I have family there." She lied, and so easily you'd think she knew what she was doing. Well, she *could* have family there for all she knew. She'd only met her aunt and uncle once years ago and never got to meet her maternal grandparents at all. She'd often joked that her mother had been spawned by Satan himself, ergo the whole no parents thing. As a teenager, that analogy had been completely palpable in Courtney's mind.

She stole a look at the baby sleeping soundly behind the driver's seat. There were blankets and pillows to confirm the conversation Courtney had overheard that morning, but she couldn't imagine how they'd all have slept in the back seat. Katie would have had to move the car seats up front, but even still, it was no wonder AJ had complained.

"Where are you guys headed?" she asked, shifting in her seat to watch Katie.

"If you're not crazy, I don't mind taking you to Toronto," she replied instead of answering Courtney's question. Katie cast her a sidelong glance. "We're headed that way."

Courtney nodded, thrilled at the idea of not having to worry for the next day where she'd hitch a ride. "Please, that'd be amazing. I–I don't have money on me now, but I promise, one day I'll pay you back and more."

"This is me being a good Samaritan and all that shit," Katie muttered, checking the rear-view before switching lanes. Her eyes bored into Courtney's. "I never get to be on the other side, so let me enjoy it. Just, I dunno, help someone else out someday."

Courtney couldn't hold back the grin. "I promise I will."

Their conversation died off, and after a while Katie pushed the power button on the radio. Listening to the soft country vocals had Courtney dozing off, and for once she couldn't remember dreaming. The sound of the baby crying woke her some time later, and a quick look out the window told her they had pulled into a rest stop. She yawned, not remembering the last time she'd slept so soundly.

"Is she okay?" Courtney asked, her voice still heavily masked with sleep. Her split lip was tender, like she'd had it pressed into the doorframe as she slept. She twisted around to see Katie in the back seat between her two kids and trying to soothe her daughter.

"She didn't feel good at breakfast ... wasn't eating much..." Katie said distractedly. She darted her gaze up to Courtney, tangible concern on her face. "She has a high temp. I–I gave her the last of the Tylenol, but we'll have to stop for some more. The dose wasn't enough."

"Yeah, okay."

"Mommy, what's wrong with Carley?" AJ tugged on his mother's jacket.

Katie took a deep breath, ruffling AJ's hair before bending to kiss his forehead. "She's not feeling well, buddy. But we'll get her fixed up in no time."

Courtney's knowledge of children was limited, but she was guessing Katie didn't want to leave Carley's side. "I can drive for a while if you want."

"You will? Nah, that's too much to ask." Katie looked tired as she spoke, and Courtney was sure she'd fall asleep with the kids if someone else was driving.

Deciding, Courtney drew up her left leg and awkwardly eased it over in the driver's seat. She grabbed the steering wheel with her good arm and pulled her weight across. The arm in a sling knocked the steering wheel, and she had to bite back all the curse words dying to come out. Instead, she breathed slowly and steadily through her nose until the pain had dispersed. With challenging difficulty, she crossed her left arm over her and fumbled with turning the ignition.

Once they were on the road again, Carley settled down some, her wails shifting to whimpers and then the occasional sob. By the time Courtney was taking an exit off the highway to the nearest convenience store, all three of her new companions were fast asleep. She studied them in the rear-view, baffled as all hell at the strange day she was having; the path she was now on was perplexing. She spotted the gas station a half a block up and headed for it, making sure she checked over her shoulder before merging into the turning lane. She'd had enough fender-benders under her belt — the last thing she wanted to do was tip Katie off that she was a shitty driver. Drew would be so proud of her if she were here. She never remembered to do the shoulder check thing.

She waited for the traffic to slow before pulling into the gas station and driving right up to the front of the store. Putting the car in park took some doing, and when it was off, she didn't know what to do. Katie was still fast asleep with the kids, and she was busting to pee again. Pulling the keys out, she slipped outside and stuffed them into her pocket. She was about to close the door over when she noticed Katie's purse in the back seat near AJ's feet. She paused, wondering if it'd look like she was stealing if she took money to buy the medicine for Carley.

Yup, not even gonna go there. This was *not* her problem. *She* had enough problems.

She locked the car up and went inside for the washroom. It wasn't until she was taking care of business that she realized Katie could've had a pad or tampon on her. Luckily, there was a coin machine with tampons for sale, and she used the last of her change on one.

She browsed the store after she was done in the washroom, and when she came across the infant Tylenol, she considered stealing it for Katie. She was broke, and it didn't take a genius to figure out Katie wasn't much better off. She even picked up the small box and glanced around to see who was around. She noticed the giant surveillance mirror on the ceiling in the corner of the store and chickened out. She had too much to lose if she got caught, and she couldn't lie to save her life.

Courtney returned to the car, feeling guilty when she spotted the baby through the front window, wailing once more. Katie had Carley in her lap in the passenger seat, unsuccessfully trying to soothe her. The little girl's cheeks and throat were flushed and sweaty.

"I changed her bum while you were in the store, and she hasn't stopped crying yet," Katie tensely supplied. Her eyebrows were pinched together in a thin line, worry deeply etched into the planes on her face.

"Maybe she's thirsty?" Courtney suggested, looking in on AJ. He was staying quiet in the back seat and fiddling with a Hot Wheels car. She slid into the driver's seat once more, closing the cold out and admitting, "Sorry, Katie. I was going to ... help myself to the Tylenol but couldn't go through with it."

"Help yourself?" Katie looked confused for a moment before glancing in the back at her son. She turned to Courtney. "I didn't expect that, Courtney. If you reach for my purse, I have a twenty in there."

Courtney did as she was asked, having to get out and retrieve the purse from the back because of her shoulder. She handed the bag to Katie.

"Thanks. And yeah, she's drinking some, but not enough to bring down this temp," Katie said. She pulled out the bill and held it for Courtney to take. "I know you just met us, but would you mind going in to buy it? I don't really wanna leave her."

Courtney nodded, grateful she now had a job to do. She returned to the store, grabbing the medicine and a bunch of paper towels. When Carley got the Tylenol into her, Katie wetted the paper towel and placed the pieces carefully onto her forehead and cheeks. The poor sweetie. She was hot all over, right down to her toes.

As Courtney waited for Katie to calm Carley down, her thoughts strayed to Cadence, Kris and Drew's precious baby girl, the only baby ever to steal her heart. She'd had two incredible parents one morning, and by noon that same day she'd lost them both. Life was so fucking cruel, it made her sick sometimes.

"I have to pee," AJ announced.

"So do I, buddy; just let me put the baby back in her seat, and I'll take you, okay?" Katie murmured, lifting Carley up. She bundled her with a blanket before transferring her into the back again. She hesitated, catching Courtney's gaze, and she could see what it cost Katie to ask her next question. "I must be crazy, but can you keep an eye on her while we run in?"

Courtney shooed her comment away. "Consider it done. I'm just grateful I'm not walking anymore. I owe you and will help any way I can."

They'd driven a few hours, but despite snacks and drinks being offered, Carley remained in agony. When Courtney suggested she go the hospital, Katie shrugged it off, saying so long as they kept liquids in her and cool clothes on her skin, she'd get better.

Hearing the child in pain was tearing at Courtney. Anxiety burrowed inside her, and she couldn't figure out why Katie wasn't taking her to see a doctor. They were stopped for food and another bathroom break when she did the only thing she could think of.

She called mama Jen.

Her heart was hammering in her chest as she waited for Drew and Melanie's mom to pick up. She hadn't spoken with Jennifer since the funeral, wasn't even sure she'd take Courtney's call. Then... "Hello?"

Courtney froze at the sound of her voice, certain the bottom of her stomach had just fallen out. Jennifer had been the type of mother she'd always dreamed of having when she was a kid.

"M-mama Jen," she sputtered, rolling her eyes at how pathetic she sounded. She let out a breath. "It's Courtney. I called 'cause ... I have a little girl who needs help."

"Courtney? Oh my God! Is it really you?" she cried.

Courtney nodded. "Hi, yes, it's me. I can't stay on the line long, and please don't tell anyone you talked with me. Jen? I'm begging you."

The audible sniffles coming through the phone almost broke Courtney. She gave a hard swallow. She noticed Katie and the kids walking across the parking lot and knew she didn't have much time. "I'm travelling with a family, and there's a one-year-old with a high fever. Over a hundred, I think, but the mother won't go to the hospital for some reason. What can we do for her to bring down the fever?"

"Ugh…" Jennifer paused, like she was considering options. "Have you given her Tylenol? And plenty of fluids, popsicles, anything she'll take. Make sure she's comfortable in her clothing; loose is better. A lukewarm bath would be best, but sponge baths if that's all you can do. If her fever hasn't gone down in twenty-four hours, then get her to the hospital, Courtney."

"Thanks, mama Jen," she croaked. Tears blurred her vision, and she rushed to wipe them away. "I'm sorry. About disappearing."

"I'm just glad you're okay. It's good to hear from you, Courtney. We've been missing you something awful and hope you'll make it home to us." Jennifer's voice was low, thick with pain. She'd lost her husband and daughter in the span of a few years and then took full custody of her granddaughter.

"Likewise."

"We love you, Courtney."

"Thanks, you too. I've gotta go now." She hung up just as the car door was opening. She wiped more tears from her eyes and watched as the little boy climbed in. "Is your belly full, AJ?"

"Yeah!" he chirped happily. He was holding a different toy this time. "I ate a burger, and they gave me a special toy!"

Night fell, and as Courtney drove down the pitch-black highway, her fear for Carley increased. Her fever was steady at a hundred and four, and now she had diarrhea. Courtney relayed what Jennifer had said to Katie, and they'd done everything but give her a bath, and still nothing. She needed to be hooked up to IV or something, and it was that thought that had Courtney following road signs to the hospital as soon as she entered Toronto. Her new friends were asleep in the back once more, so if all went well Katie wouldn't notice until it was too late to turn back. She understood domestic disputes — if that's what was going on — but putting a child in danger was crossing all sorts of lines.

"Katie," Courtney quietly called as she pulled into an emergency parking space. She shut off the car, pocketing the keys before shifting her aching body in the seat. Driving so many hours hadn't helped her to heal whatsoever after the fight. She watched the trio, realizing there was so much she didn't know about Katie, but it didn't matter. The mother had good inside her, Courtney could feel it with her whole being. Whatever she was experiencing couldn't have been her doing; Courtney refused to believe otherwise.

"Katie, wake up," she called again, gently shaking her awake. When Katie's eyes opened, Courtney put on her best apologetic face and gestured to the hospital. "I don't know a lot about you and the kids, but I'd like to. You seem like a good person, Katie, so whatever you're going through, know it's not worth Carley."

Katie gave a hard swallow, glancing out the window and saying hoarsely, "My husband will find us if we check into the hospital. He always finds us. I was ... trying to get away."

She knew it; Katie was fleeing from an abusive relationship. Courtney took her hand and squeezed. "He won't make it before Carley is fixed up and you're on the move again. You can leave as soon as she's better. And as soon as I'm home in B.C. again, I'll help any way that I can if you need me."

Katie gave a slight nod, tension tightening her shoulders. Tears glimmered in her eyes. "You're a good person, Courtney. I'm glad I picked you up. I never pick up hitchhikers."

Courtney smiled, believing that statement and glad she made an exception. "Ready?"

"No, but I'm doing it anyway."

"Yes, you are."

Chapter 7

Toronto, ON, March 14

COURTNEY PUSHED OPEN THE door to the tattoo parlour, and the bells hanging over the archway jangled as she crossed the threshold, her heavy duffel bag bouncing off her shoulder. A gentle gust of warm air greeted her from an oil rad as she stepped inside, effectively taking the chill off her snow-covered jacket. She glanced around the small studio, unsure if she should be taking her boots off or not. It was empty in the front area, so she didn't have anything to go by.

"Hello?"

"I'm just closing up!" a woman's voice called from the backroom.

"Oh, um," Courtney replied, setting her duffel bag on the floor and glancing at the slip of paper where she'd written down the name and address at the local library. "Lexi? It's Lexi, right? You're the owner?"

A woman stepped out of the back room, a takeout dish in one hand and a plastic fork in the other. Courtney cocked an eyebrow and watched her casually dig into her food and take another bite, all the while not taking her eyes off her new customer. She had Courtney getting serious Ruby Rose vibes. The person before her was of average height, lean, dressed in black leather pants, a black t-shirt with the tattoo shop's logo, Cole's Creations, on the front and three chains around her neck. She had piercings in her ears, lip, and nose, and both arms had an entire tattoo sleeve. A collage of designs and handwriting were tattooed along her neck, and a long-stemmed outlined rose on the back of one hand. She had full lips, and the heavy outliner made her baby blues pop more. There were two small tattoos on her face — a feather along her hairline, and *Lex* handwritten under her left eye. She didn't even look like Ruby Rose, but that same confident sex appeal was pouring out of her.

For the first time since she'd left Van, an old familiar burn spread through Courtney. The sudden, almost aggressive lust had her fumbling on her next words. "I–I'm Corey. I'd called earlier? Sorry I'm late. I got lost."

Lexi — or the person Courtney assumed was Lexi — came closer, close enough that Courtney spotted the tongue piercing as she spoke. "What's your real name?"

Courtney faltered, losing her train of thought. She was breathless all of a sudden. Fuck, the tongue ring was hot. She'd never been with anyone with one, and now she couldn't help but wonder how damn good it'd feel pressing against her aching nub. Mel used to joke that she was a sex addict, and back before Drew dying and Courtney committing to Natalie again, there was a time when she wondered if her friend was right. If it was true, then she'd had one hell of a long dry spell, and it was no wonder she was practically climbing out of her clothes.

"E—excuse me?"

Lexi shrugged, moving past Courtney to lock the parlour door. She closed the blinds as well. "You don't look like a Corey, so I'm taking a wild guess it's not your real name."

Courtney flushed, pissed off she was being so reactive to someone she'd never see again. It wasn't like her to be speechless, and she chalked it up to not having had sex for almost a year. She watched Lexi take one more bite before tossing the takeout container in the garbage. Her hair was black, with blue strands running through it. It wasn't short or long; rather, it fell haphazardly in layers around her ears, with some pieces reaching her sensual jawline.

"My name is Courtney," she admitted, licking her dry lips. She really had gotten lost, since there were three other tattoo shops on the same block. Lexi's was the only shop that did drop-ins, and it'd taken some time to figure out which was hers. As it turned out, she didn't manoeuvre around the city as well without wheels. Since the scare with Carley, Katie had fled with the kids once again, convinced her husband would find them. Subsequently, Courtney had picked up odd jobs and slept in various places and got lost countless times. "I don't mind paying extra, if you'll still do me." She realized too late what she'd said, and by the flare of interest in Lexi's eyes, she'd realized it too.

The tattooist grinned, rubbing her tongue ring over her bottom lip as if she were blatantly considering it. She headed for the front counter, pulling a waiver out from the first drawer. "Let's start with the tat first. If you don't pass out from it, then we can talk payment."

"What? Oh, I didn't mean ... I'm not like ... so not what I meant at all." Horny. She was horny, that's what she meant. An awkward laugh escaped Courtney, and she went over to the counter as well.

Lexi chuckled, sliding the waiver toward her. "I know what you meant. Fill this out, okay? And you said on the phone you had an idea of a design?"

Courtney nodded, taking the pen offered before glancing over the waiver. It asked a lot of personal things, questions she either didn't have an answer to or didn't want to divulge. She hesitated, the pen hovering over her address. "I um, don't have a permanent place at the moment, hence the bags. Doing some soul-searching, you know?" At any rate, she probably shouldn't be telling random strangers she was basically homeless — *especially* not if someone was indeed following her. Street-savvy she was not, but she was learning. Sort of.

"That's fine, just sign and date it, and you know, feel free to leave your number."

Courtney didn't miss the innuendo in Lexi's voice, and she was buzzing inside as she quickly jotted down the date. Besides sex, fighting was the only thing that seemed to curb her hunger for stress relief and the endorphins she so craved. She was bouncing off the walls waiting for her damn shoulder to heal, so sex with a hot girl sounded just like what the doctor ordered.

Even so, Courtney was only planning to be in Toronto for another couple of weeks. She didn't know Lexi, couldn't guarantee she wouldn't fall hard, and one thing she did know was she was too psychologically damaged to be in a relationship. The last girl she'd kissed, she would've married had things not gone south.

She signed her name, dropping the pen down to grab her bag and follow Lexi into the back room. The tattooing area was spacious and sanitary, with two chairs next to a laptop and printer, a La-Z-Boy in the corner, and what looked like a massage table. The blue disposable bed liner and pillow appeared new, as if Lexi had just put them on before Courtney got there. She was nervous about getting her first tattoo. She never thought she'd be getting one without at least one of her best friends by her side. Then again, she never thought she'd have gone ten months without talking to Mel over the phone, but she did. To this day, Drew's fraternal twin had no clue where Courtney had been or what she'd been doing since she left their hometown. She was certain whatever Mel concocted, Courtney underground fighting wouldn't be it.

"So, what design do you have? Or are you wanting to check out the flash sheets I've got hanging out front?" Lexi asked, pulling Courtney's train of thought back to the present.

Courtney blinked, then remembered she had the design she'd scribbled down stuffed in her backpack. She pulled the bag off her shoulder and noticed she still had her heavy jacket on. Wow, she was doing a stellar job acting like a complete idiot tonight.

Clearing her throat, she silently passed the sheet to Lexi before stripping off her plaid suede. "Can you do it? I know I'm keeping you here late, but I'd be grateful if you could. I was thinking on my ribs."

"Well, yeah, I mean, I can definitely do it. It's nice..." Lexi slowly replied, studying the design a moment longer before meeting Courtney's gaze. "With the flock of birds and the feather, it might be too much on your ribs.

It'd probably take away from the script itself. Personally, when I do rib tats, I like keeping it simpler. Are you set on the location? I mean, whatever, it's your body. You can take my advice or leave it."

"Okay. Well, I definitely want it on my ribs, so what did you have in mind?" Courtney asked, her interest piqued as she watched Lexi swivel around in her chair. She wasn't dead set on the design she'd come up with. She'd spent the better part of her morning at the library scrolling through Google images and then finally coming up with the script she wanted and a bird design from another image. She couldn't find any on the ribs with pictures she liked, and maybe Lexi's reasoning was bang-on. Just having the script might make it more visually appealing.

"It's a memorial piece, right? What date did they die?" Lexi wondered, not lifting her head as she sketched a design into her iPad. She was hovered over it, and the tattoo on the back of her neck made Courtney wonder where it stopped on her skin. Lexi seemed like a woman who'd have no problem inking her entire back.

"Yeah, uh, for my best friend," Courtney murmured. She swallowed, "Last year. May 6, 2018." She didn't divulge more, and Lexi didn't ask her to. Talking about Drew pained her more than getting the shit kicked out of her in the ring. Her physical wounds always healed over time, but the internal wound she'd suffered from Drew being snatched away kept closing and reopening. Like a goddamn door — no matter how fucking hard she tried, she couldn't slam that shit shut inside her.

"Is that your natural eye colour?"

The rough subject change caught Courtney off guard, but perhaps Lexi knew she was once again a prisoner of her thoughts and was trying to distract her. She eyed up the artwork on the walls, slow to respond. "It is. You aren't the first person to ask." And no doubt would she be the last. Courtney's blueish green hues were her most discernable feature, after you factored in her mass of red curls. Their color changed to an almost jade when she was upset and lightened to a celeste shade of blue when she was happy.

She met Lexi's gaze. "They're crazy sexy. I think they've changed colour three times since you walked in here."

Her ballsy comment had Courtney grinning, feeling more confident than before. She leaned back in the chair, crossing one long leg over the other. A satisfied feeling coursed through her when Lexi's gaze dropped down to follow the movement.

Hell, yeah, she still had it.

"I bet you fuck half your clientele with those pickup lines."

Lexi grinned, not bothering to hide the fact she was checking Courtney out. She turned back to her iPad. "The female half, maybe. But don't worry," she added with a wink, "I'm clean."

Courtney didn't know how to reply to that, so she sat there in silence while Lexi finished up her sketch. The offer was on the table, but her heart wasn't in it, and damn it all to hell, but she missed having her heart in sync with her raging sex drive. She missed mattering to someone.

"What do you think of this?"

Courtney glanced up to see Lexi holding the iPad out for her to take. She did, leaning back in the chair once more to study the custom work. She was impressed; the font style had been brought more to life now. It was a bold, outlined handwritten font with stylized wisps on the uppercase letters. On the right side of the script there were two small red hearts, and underneath in numerical format was the date Drew died.

Courtney's throat constricted as she stared at the image. The lump lodged there was hard to push down when she swallowed. "It's stunning. Can you, um, add her birthdate too?"

Lexi's face softened, giving her entire badass look the warmth it was lacking. She reached over to catch a runaway tear on Courtney's cheek. "Hey, don't cry, beautiful girl."

Courtney's eyes drifted closed, eagerly soaking in the comfort of Lexi's touch. She couldn't help it; it'd been a long ass time since she'd felt anything other than a kick or a punch to her skin. She didn't realize before now how much she'd missed the intimacy.

"Fuck, I'm sorry," she muttered, turning her face away as her cheeks flushed. "Breaking down wasn't my intention. I just wanted something to remember her by."

Lexi gently swivelled Courtney's chair around to face her again, standing up to rest both her hands on either armrest, effectively blocking her in. Courtney's startled gaze flew up to meet the sympathy in Lexi's. "What?"

"I'm gonna kiss you, beautiful girl, unless you stop me," she murmured, inching her face closer and zeroing in on Courtney's parted lips.

Courtney swallowed, drowning in Lexi's blue depths. She closed her eyes, tears still seeping out the corners. "That's bold of you to say."

"I disagree." Lexi's lips grazed her hairline before planting a soft kiss on Courtney's forehead. "You've been eye-fucking me since you walked in here; I just beat you to the punch."

Courtney blushed; it was the truth, so she didn't bother denying what was so obvious. She breathed in Lexi's masculine scent, the heady body spray she had on giving off hints of deep woods and caramel and coconut. Fuck, she was a goner.

Lexi inched closer still, and Courtney opened her eyes in time to see her smouldering gaze. "I'm gonna kiss you now. You have until three, two, one..."

Chapter 8

COURTNEY'S EYES DRIFTED CLOSED when Lexi's lips brushed hers. Hooking up with random strangers wasn't new to her, and yet with the electricity crackling in the air, it felt both thrilling and nerve-wracking. The pulse in her throat was wild with abandon as she angled her face into Lexi's passionate kiss; the ring in her bottom lip pressed against Courtney's, but it wasn't long before she hardly felt it at all. Lexi's soft, almost delicate, artistic fingers came up to swipe away the remaining tears on her cheeks before cupping her face to deepen the kiss.

Courtney's own hands were roaming, sliding up Lexi's arms to sink one into her thick black locks and the other around her shoulder. She moaned when Lexi's tongue slid seductively over her lips, silently asking for entrance. Courtney obliged, opening her mouth and distractedly thinking the gentleness in Lexi was surprising and yet did nothing to curb her appeal. That pierced tongue stroked Courtney's, the small but present metal ball applying pressure down the centre as it made its way toward her throat. Then it was swirling around her tongue, the barbell dragging behind, trapping it in a sinuous circle of sensitivity. Courtney was buzzing; whatever upset she'd felt before was long gone now that she was being held and masterfully, dizzily kissed.

When the kiss broke, Lexi ran her tongue along Courtney's bottom lip, then nipped her chin. She started blazing a trail of hot kisses down her throat, and Courtney's head lolled back. "Are you so thorough with all your conquests?" she gasped as Lexi's hand slid down her body to cup her breast through her shirt.

Lexi lifted her mouth from Courtney's collarbone, her eyes laughing. "What conquests? I only see you. Courtney with no permanent address, but with eyes so sinful and a smile so sad, you could make literally *anybody* drop their panties to please you."

A giggle escaped Courtney; the sound was so strange coming from her. She wasn't a giggly kind of girl, but she'd also never hooked up with a Ruby Rose-level sexy before. "I came here for a tattoo," she reminded Lexi, drawing her back in for another kiss. She left the chair to reach for the hem of Lexi's t-shirt, pulling it over head. Her earlier assumption of Lexi's addiction to tattoos was correct. Intricate patterns covered her sides and stomach, leaving just under her small naked breasts bare up to her collarbone, where her neck tattoo began. On her back there was a huge panther coming out of a bush. Courtney never thought she'd be attracted to someone with so much ink, and yet here she was, exuberantly stripping off her own shirt.

Lexi reached around her to unsnap Courtney's bra, a hot look in her eyes as she pulled it off her shoulders. "Don't tell me you're an ink virgin," she murmured, sounding incredulous as she explored Courtney's body with her hands. Lexi's fingers lingered over Courtney's toned tummy and pierced navel, and then her mouth closed over her breasts, sucking one stiffened peak into her mouth at a time.

Courtney hissed, her fingers delving back into Lexi's hair as she switched between suckling and dragging her barbell across her nipples. Her thong was soaked through, had been as soon as she'd set eyes on Lexi, and it was a likely possibility Courtney would come just by her doing this. Lexi must have had the same idea, because the next thing Courtney knew, her jeans were being unfastened and pulled down to her ankles. She helped Lexi remove her winter boots and jeans, and as soon as she freed herself from the bundle of clothes, Lexi was lifting one of Courtney's feet up to rest on the chair.

"Fuck, you're hot. And so wet for me," Lexi gushed, swiping her hand over the drenched thong covering her mound. She straightened, kissing Courtney again and pushing aside the fabric to slide a long finger between her folds.

Courtney bucked against her hand, groaning into Lexi's kiss and not wanting to be the only one being fucked. Her pulse was racing as she tugged Lexi closer so they were hip to hip. She started to slip her hand into the waistband of Lexi's leathers, but she wasn't having it. Instead she pulled away from Courtney's mouth, giving her a devilish grin before dropping down on one knee. Pushing aside the ruined panties, she quickly replaced her fingers with her studded tongue.

"Shit," Courtney cursed, caught between wanting Lexi to either slow down or pick up the pace. She whimpered, eyes glazing over as Lexi's tongue tortured her aching nub, and she couldn't believe she'd gone a year without sex. She must have been fucking crazy.

When Lexi paused a moment later to literally rip apart her thong, Courtney probably should have been scared, or at least apprehensive, that she was letting this stranger do whatever to her, but she was too busy soaring high on her dopamine rush. And when Lexi inserted not two, but three fingers inside her at the same time she was sucking and biting her hypersensitive clit, Courtney cried out and came harder than she even knew was possible.

Her legs were trembling, her pussy still clenching around Lexi's fingers, and all she could do to hold herself up was grip her lover's shoulders. Lexi didn't seem to be in a rush to leave her place between Courtney's thighs, because she licked and ate until the last spasm had passed. Only then did she slowly pull away, deliberately watching Courtney's reaction.

"That was insane," Courtney breathed, unable to miss the fatigue creeping into her senses now. She peered down at Lexi, giving her a soft smile. "Thank you."

"Seemed like you needed the distraction. And you definitely needed the attention. You shouldn't let yourself get so strung out. Sex is good for our mental health," Lexi quietly stated, the corners of her lips tilting up. She held Courtney's hand as she dropped her leg back down to sit once more in the chair. Courtney reached for her, guilty the sex had been so one-sided, but when she touched Lexi, all the girl did was direct her hand to her breasts. "Not now. Let me give you your very first ink, and then after, you can give me all the payment you want."

"How do you make any money with terms like those?" Courtney wondered, laughing lightly. She traced her thumb over Lexi's nipple, watching with lazy curiosity as it hardened under her touch.

"Well, maybe, *just* maybe, I consider it a potential investment," Lexi replied, pulling away to locate her shirt on the floor. Courtney examined the panther staring at her from Lexi's back. It was so alive, like it was ready to jump out at her.

"What do you mean?"

Lexi pulled her shirt back on and headed over to her desk once more to pick up her iPad. "You won't find a single person out there saying tattoos aren't addicting. So, here's hoping you'll be back for another one."

"You don't even know me," Courtney said, pulling on her jeans and bra. She didn't bother with her shirt, since she was about to be tattooed.

"Sorry to bring it up again, but what should I put for a birthdate?"

Courtney sobered some, stepping behind Lexi to wrap her arms around her shoulders. She kissed her cheek, closing her eyes as Drew's wide smile illuminated inside her frontal lobe. Apparently, when a loved one passed, the first thing you forgot about them was the sound of their voice. No one had bothered to give her a heads-up, and when it'd started happening months later, she'd found herself scrambling to find old videos of Drew on Facebook. The videos she thought she'd taken that night at the club had turned out to be fuzzy, drunken pictures. She'd almost gone home right then and there, determined to ask Jennifer to help her look for some. She probably would have if she hadn't succeeded going the Facebook route, and now every night before she went to sleep, she listened to Drew daring her and Melanie to a swim race. She didn't want to ever forget the sound of her voice. "Put, um…" Her voice wobbled, and she paused. Fuck, she thought she could do this. Taking a deep breath, she began again. "December 23, 1995."

"I'm sorry about your friend, Courtney," Lexi murmured, turning her face to give her a gentle kiss.

"Thank you."

When Lexi was finished adding the date, she printed off the design and then scanned the paper into some sort of stencil machine. It came out looking like a temporary tattoo sheet. Courtney unwrapped herself from Lexi so the artist could wash her hands and get her tattooing station set up. She was a true professional, wearing black latex gloves and keeping a very sanitary table of instruments, and Courtney watched as everything went into slip bags of some sort. To keep from getting blood and germs on the tools, she supposed.

Courtney was lying down on the table when Lexi spoke again. She could hear the latex gloves coming off and fresh ones going on. "It occurs to me you might wanna reconsider putting it somewhere else. People don't generally put their first ink on their ribs, 'cause it hurts more than other places."

Courtney shook her head, turning onto her side. "I'm not afraid of the pain. Can't be worse than a dislocated shoulder."

Lexi looked impressed, maybe even a little hot for her, but she said nothing as she disinfected Courtney's skin before placing the stencil on overtop. Their eyes met, and excitement fluttered through Courtney. "You look sexy as fuck," Lexi stated, sounding all too ready for Courtney to make her first payment.

As Lexi got to work, Courtney relaxed her head on the pillow and focused on her surroundings to try to distract her mind from the needle digging into her flesh. Pictures lined the walls of Lexi with various people and various hair styles, or clients flaunting their fresh ink Lexi had done. There was an article up about her opening her new shop two years ago.

"What made you want to become a tattoo artist?"

The tugging stopped momentarily. "It was always a possibility. My pops was one, so he got me into the scene. I worked with him for a bit, but uh, when he died, I relocated the business. Kept the same name, though."

Something sounded off, like half the details were missing. Courtney grimaced as the needle hit the tender spot where her rib had bruised during her last match. "I'm so sorry, Lexi. How'd he die?"

For a long while, the only sounds were the ones coming from the tattoo gun. She didn't think Lexi would answer her, but then she surprised her by saying very low, "His shop was burned down one night, with him in it. Investigators said he'd been handcuffed to a desk; everyone thinks it was gang-related."

"God, that's awful." Courtney didn't know what else to say. It sounded like something out of a mafia movie, not happening to someone she was getting to know. Then she surprised herself by adding hoarsely, "My best friend's name was Drew. She was murdered too. Right in front of me."

"Fuck, Courtney, that's brutal. How ... I mean, why?" Lexi didn't lift her hands from her work but paused long enough to press a kiss to her hip.

Tears pricked Courtney's eyes, and it wasn't because of the needle digging into her ribs. She swallowed. "Her fiancé had been part of a gang of sorts. Not a huge organized one or anything, but a handful of sorry-ass criminals who did a lot of shit to support their drug habit. Well, the leader came back to settle a score and, uh, Drew purposely got in the way. She blocked the psychopath with the knife from reaching Kris and their daughter, and so he killed her instead."

"Damn."

Courtney wiped her tears away. "Right out in the open, too. In the middle of a fucking marathon and not a care in the world." She shook her head, adding, "I'm sorry. I shouldn't be pouring my heart out to you."

"Oh man, I actually heard about that last year," Lexi said with genuine sympathy. "It was on the news. In B.C., right? The dude went nuts, stabbed her like ten times with a hunting knife."

"Thirteen," Courtney sniffled, wishing she hadn't brought it up. It wasn't something *anyone* should talk about, let alone her. It felt disrespectful to Drew. Was she so hard up for a connection, she'd blurt out the first awful personal thing she could think of?

Silence stretched out between them. It wasn't an uneasy silence; rather, Courtney was lost now in her thoughts, and Lexi was concentrating on her tattoo. She must have been tired, since it was going on eleven, but she never complained. Now that they weren't talking, every pull of the needle was starting to get to Courtney. The pain was worth it; it was a beautiful kind of pain and not as agonizing as when she'd dislocated her shoulder.

"Okay, I'm moving on to shading in the hearts; should only take a few minutes. It's gonna hurt more, but apparently pain is your thing." She heard humour in Lexi's voice, and the fact she was trying to comfort Courtney made her feel a little better. "So, will you be in the city for a while? We could grab a bite or something some evening."

The tone in her voice was indiscernible, but Courtney still felt she needed to set boundaries, and quickly. The last thing she needed was another failed relationship. "I'm not sticking around, Lexi," she said with firm grit. She was putting her foot down about this. "What's going on with us isn't gonna last, so don't go falling for me, okay? I'm not a good person to be tied to, and eventually I'll stop running and go home."

Lexi chuckled. "So you think I'm a U-Haul lesbian. Geez, tell me how you really feel. And while we're on the subject, quite frankly, you don't have enough ink for my kind of U-Haul. You'd have to come back at least ... three more times before I started falling for you. So relax, beautiful girl, I only wanted to know what your plans are while you're here, not for the rest of your life."

That had Courtney laughing outright. She wasn't stupid; she knew in her vulnerable state she could easily fall for the likes of Lexi. "And I'm bi — I don't prefer one sex over the other." She winced, having to pause just to breathe through the needle scraping over the same spot as before. Fuck, what if she'd done more than bruise her rib?

"Yeah, okay, no. That's a deal-breaker right there," Lexi joked. The gun shut off, and Courtney felt her patting the fresh tattoo again. "I'm just cleaning up the excess ink and blood. How you holding up?"

"Honestly?" Courtney asked and dug deep down for a self-evaluation. She felt tired and a bit woozy. "I could use water and some sugar."

"I should've asked if you ate before you came here. You're probably faint. Let me get you covered, and I'll grab something out of the fridge."

"Thank you," Courtney replied, appreciating her thoughtfulness. Lexi gently covered her tattoo with aftercare cream before ripping off a large piece of transparent adhesive tape. Once it was secured over Courtney's ribs, she stripped off her gloves once more.

Her hand rested on Courtney's hip. "Don't get up just yet. I'll be right back with food."

When she appeared crouched down before Courtney a few minutes later, she had a glass of water with a straw in one hand and a wrapped Twinkie in the other. She held the straw up to Courtney's lips. "The fridge was empty, so you're stuck with this for now. Take a drink."

Courtney did, taking a long sip and licking her dry lips. Then she took a few bites of Twinkie before she teased, "Look at you go. It's like we're on a date. You've fed me, entertained and talked with me, plus we had sex. Tonight turned out even better then I'd planned."

Lexi flicked her tongue ring across her bottom lip. She seemed to toy with the barbell out of habit, and it was seriously turning Courtney on. "What can I say? I get off on pleasing gorgeous women," she said with a playful grin.

That had Courtney rolling her eyes. "You are *such* a guy." She was feeling better, having finished the Twinkie and half the water. She sat up slowly, very aware of the slight pull in her skin where her new art was embedded. She caught her reflection in the mirror on the wall. "Wow. Looks awesome, Lex."

"You like it?" Lexi confirmed, checking Courtney's side to make sure the adhesive was on flat. When she straightened, she leaned into her for another kiss. Courtney didn't mind; in fact, she found she was reluctant to leave.

She'd felt isolated for so long, and she despised sleeping alone. She'd always been that way, and of course the therapist inside Natalie had always found it strange considering Courtney was an only child. At home, she used to sleep with either her body pillow pressing into her back or the giant teddy the twins had bought her one Christmas.

"I do. You did a great job. Thank you," she murmured, splaying her hand across Lexi's cheek and returning her kiss.

Lexi reached up to graze the scar tissue on her eyebrow. "Infected piercing?"

Courtney shook her head, slipping her hands under Lexi's t-shirt. Her fingers roamed over her soft skin while she answered, "Fighting. I kickbox."

Her fingers reached Lexi's hardened nipples, but before she could toy with them, Lexi grabbed her hands, stilling her. She was practically vibrating, she was so horny. She took a couple of deep breaths before saying, "Let me clean up my station. Where were you planning to crash tonight? It's getting late. You can stay with me the night if you want, and I swear I won't expect a U-Haul come tomorrow. I don't even want one. There's too many ladies out there to settle on just one."

Courtney considered her offer, knowing it made the most sense. Better than the hostel she was heading back to, and it came with a sleeping partner. "Okay," she agreed, "so long as you let me pay my end of the deal in cash, not sex."

Lexi looked confused. "So you wanna crash and not hook up?"

Courtney smiled, pulling her in for another long kiss, eager to feel the barbell again. "Oh, I plan on hooking up. I'm more than ready for more sex with you."

Chapter 9

Chasing me through the crowd, he's after me. I need him after me; that way, I can distract him from Drew and Kris. I feel his hot, stale breath on my neck one second, and then he's disappeared. He's nowhere, and then I'm yelping as I feel rough fingers grabbing at my sleeve.

He's after me, and I'm pushing past so many people, but they can't hear me screaming; they can't feel my hands shoving against him. He's coming close now; I listen to his pants in the misty air. Not paying attention, I trip, falling down, down, down. I tumble to the pavement, scraping my hands and knees, and as I do this I'm turning to see where he's gone.

He's before me, black hoodie obscuring his sinister features. It's the long, hunting knife gleaming in midair that catches my attention. He's captured me, I think mindlessly in the last moment.

A horror-filled scream stretches my mouth wide when the knife strikes.

"Hey, hey, beautiful girl, it's okay. You're safe, you're at my place," a soothing voice crooned, breaking the vicious barrier of Courtney's mind. Comforting arms wrapped around her, tender lips brushing the spot under her earlobe. She sighed, aware of her racing pulse, aware of Lexi spooning her under the sheets in her cozy, innocuous queen-size bed.

"A queen size for all my queens, 'cause you know, a double isn't enough space for all the things I like to do with a girl."

"You had a nightmare, but you're safe here. No one's gonna hurt you," Lexi continued to whisper, nuzzling her face into the crook of Courtney's neck.

Courtney expelled a long, drawn-out breath. When her heartbeat was halfway normal, she asked in the darkness, "What's your reasoning for not having a king-size bed? All your 'queens' sleeping too far away?"

Lexi chuckled, her warm breath fanning Courtney's cheek. "It wouldn't fit up the stairs."

The corners of her mouth tilted up in a small smile, and she snuggled farther into Lexi's embrace. God, she'd missed being held. It made her feel almost safe. "Thank you, Lexi. For everything."

"You wanna talk about it?"

"It" being the nightmare, Courtney presumed, but she shook her head, turning her face to close her mouth over Lexi's. She lingered, stuck between wanting sex to help her forget the nightmare and the strong desire not to leave Lexi's arms anytime soon. She knew there wasn't a romantic future for them, but she already felt as if they would be lifelong friends. And for some reason, a friend who cared and offered comfort when she needed it was more important right then for Courtney. Sex she could get anytime, but comfort in someone's arms happened all too rarely. And so she wiggled her butt to get as close as possible to Lexi, letting out a soft sigh as Lexi's arms pulled her against her chest so her bare breasts were squashed against Courtney's back. Her face nuzzled Courtney's neck, and she could hear Lexi inhaling her scent, as if she too, needed this level of intimacy.

Even if for just tonight.

She woke hours later to soft music playing in the kitchen and the smell of fresh coffee brewing. Opening her eyes, she noticed her bags a few feet away. Lexi must have put them in the bedroom so she could get dressed. Her mood drastically brightening at her new friend's thoughtfulness, Courtney slipped out of bed on the hunt for clean clothes. On the way to her duffel bag, she caught sight of her naked form in the full-length mirror beside Lexi's closet. It was one of those old-fashioned, standalone mirrors in the frame; Courtney was quickly finding out Lexi had many layers, and a love of old things was one of them. Take her apartment. She owned it, since it was situated above her tattoo shop. She'd bought the small, 1940s duplex and converted the bottom half into her shop. There was even an old-fashioned clawfoot tub in the spacious bathroom she'd refinished herself.

Her tattoo looked well, from what she could see. She'd have thought the adhesive would've torn apart during their sexual escapade. A wondering giggle left her as she bent to zip open her duffel bag. Courtney had only been with three other women, and as good as Natalie had been in the bedroom, she didn't even compare to Lexi. Lexi was on an entirely different level of hotness. She had a thing for toys, some naughty, some nice, and some downright kinky. Needless to say, Lexi was at the top of Courtney's list of exquisite bed partners. Really, it was like eating the cake and having it too.

She chose the baggiest of her two sweaters, as per Lexi's suggestion, and her sole pair of low-riding camo cargos. Less feminine than she'd allowed in her old life, but Courtney had long since learned to appreciate the casual outfits.

She tucked the clothes under her arm and grabbed her makeup and toiletry bag as well. She was on her way out of the bedroom when she thought to cover herself. She located a towel draped across an ottoman in the corner, wrapping it around carefully before she continued out to the rest of the apartment. She found Lexi pouring waffles into a maker next to the stove, her back to Courtney. She looked already showered and sporting another punk style today, wearing a spiked belt through tight black jeans that had rips in the back against her thighs, and a snug black muscle shirt, large enough around the arms that Courtney could see right through to the other side. Her sports bra was also black, and every tattoo along her sides was visible from one angle or another. She completed the ensemble with a rather vintage black gangster hat. The clothes made her slight body hella fine, but

Courtney knew she herself would never pull off a look like that due to her curves.

"I hope you eat breakfast. I know I can't start the day without scarfing something sweet down."

"Sure, please," Courtney replied, hearing her stomach growl at just the mention of food. "I'm starving. I think the Twinkie was all I had since lunch yesterday."

Lexi turned around to tsk in Courtney's direction. "You'd think a person would at least google what to do before getting inked. You're lucky you didn't pass out."

"I'm tougher than I look," Courtney replied, not missing Lexi's wandering gaze. She cleared her throat. "Is it okay if I use your shower?"

Lexi headed toward her in three easy strides, the rips in the front of her jeans flashing pale skin as she moved. The chains around her neck were back in place this morning, as were her skater shoes. She stopped right in front of Courtney, and for a lightweight woman she could sure take up space. "First, let me see how the ink's holding up. The Hypafix is pretty versatile stuff, but it probably wasn't made for wild bed partners immediately after it's put on."

"Wild, huh?" Courtney said, grinning at her mothering. She was liking Lexi a lot. "You're looking quite fine in your hat, by the way." She set down the items in her hands before pulling apart the opening in her towel.

Lexi beamed, bending to carefully examine her ribs. "It's a 1920s fedora; I bought it online."

"Again, are you this thorough with all your conquests?" Courtney teased, watching as Lexi's fingers left her side and moved lightly over her skin. She stopped on her torso, trailing her fingers down over Courtney's abdominal muscles.

"Fuck, I can't help it. Your body's like an ivory version of fucking Wonder Woman. You must hit the gym every day."

"I never used to, but I find working out every day helps me in the cage. I haven't been able to do as much calisthenics training since I hurt my shoulder, though," Courtney replied, her breathing shallow now. She was glad to see her easily turned on sex drive hadn't left her in the past year. She needed to get away from Lexi and start thinking about her departure. Staying would only get her more attached.

"I've been thinking about that," Lexi said, seeming reluctant to stand back up. She did, however, wandering back to the stove. She dished up a plate of waffles with real maple syrup, whipped cream, and strawberries, and a mug of piping hot coffee before carrying it to the small kitchen table off to the side. She gestured for Courtney to sit.

Dumbfounded and quite aware she was standing naked in Lexi's kitchen, she snatched up the towel to wrap around herself once more. Then she sat, raising an eyebrow to Lexi's unfinished sentenced. "About?"

Lexi returned with a serving of her own, taking a seat across from her. She gestured to Courtney's right hand, where her knuckles were noticeably larger than her left because she could punch harder with her dominant side. Then she gestured to Courtney as a whole. "I think you're an underground kickboxer."

Courtney's fork stilled halfway to her mouth, and it took a second to recover her surprised expression. "Underground ... fighting?"

Lexi had the audacity to laugh. "I hope you don't play poker, 'cause you're a terrible liar. It actually makes sense you'd want to kick a bunch of ass if you're in pain. I went through similar shit after my dad. Also explains why you don't seem to have a manager keeping tabs on you and why you have two bags to your name right now. You *are* running, but also running *to* the next rush you can find."

Courtney was silent as she added milk to her coffee. "Not saying you're right, but if you were, then what do you know about it?"

Lexi held up a hand while she chewed. When she swallowed, she shrugged. "Gang affiliations, remember? I know of people that are into the underground scene. Could probably get you into a fight right here in the city."

Courtney reluctantly shook her head. She sipped her coffee, noting a hint of hazelnut in the espresso, and moaned as the liquid comfort slid down her throat. "I fucked up my shoulder in January, and according to research, I shouldn't fight until April. I'll be long gone by then."

"So, you really aren't sticking around?"

She shook her head again, keeping her gaze averted. The last thing she needed was Lexi asking her to stay. Although abso-fucking-lutely amazing in bed, she was an unexpected detour in Courtney's plans, and it would change nothing.

"Well, thought I'd give you a heads-up; I've noticed a black sedan across the street since last night. He's moved three times, and it looks like the same brown-haired guy each time. Are you being tailed? You know, if this was a movie, I'd say he looks government. You in trouble, Courtney?"

Courtney's eyes narrowed. Dammit, she thought she'd lost him. She hadn't seen or felt his presence since she'd crossed the border, truly believing she'd outsmarted him. God, it felt like she'd been on an overnight vacation from her nightmarish life, but now it was time for a heavy dose of reality. The sudden case of nerves had her pushing away her plate. "It's nothing I can't handle, Lexi, so please don't worry about me."

She'd been thinking the same thing the last few weeks. Her stalker hadn't acted stalkish, — if that was even a word, except for the night he'd broken into her apartment. But even then, he'd nursed her back to health. The only certain fact she believed anymore was someone was indeed following her.

But who? And *why*? She'd considered the idea of him being police or something as well, but then she was sure she'd already have been arrested for underground fighting. She was past fucking tired of the dramatics; he was either going to be a threat or not, but it was damn time for her to end this. Yeah, it was time for her to turn the tables and confront his ass.

Lexi got up from the table, her plate empty. She stopped next to Courtney, affectionately resting a hand on hers. "Stay here as long as you need, have a shower, do whatever. I've got a client coming in a half hour, so I gotta go."

Courtney reached up, wrapping her hand around Lexi's neck to pull her down for a kiss. "Again, thank you. I hate to impose, so I won't linger, I promise."

"I wouldn't mind you lingering a few days more. There's still those handcuffs we never got to use," Lexi said huskily against her lips.

"Ah, but then attachments would form, and neither of us are looking for a relationship," Courtney reminded her, turning back to her coffee. She took a sip, watching as Lexi took her plate to the sink and added, "I very much want to be your friend, though. I think you're kind of awesome."

"I really am, though." Lexi laughed, grabbing her cell phone and keys. She punched in the passcode. "Give me your digits, and I'll keep in touch. Might even be able to find a fight for you in a month's time."

"Here, let me." She held her hand out for the cell, quickly putting in her number before giving it back. She stood up to give Lexi a hug goodbye. "I sent myself a text, so now I have yours too."

"Okay, sweet. Well, hey, take care of yourself and keep in touch."

"I will, and same to you." Courtney pulled away, feeling desolate as she watched Lexi go. It was for the best, it really was.

Honestly.

And yet by the time she'd showered and washed the few dishes Lexi had left dirty in the sink, Courtney found herself shooting her a text message and wondering if they could hang later. Turns out she wasn't ready to let this enlivened feeling end so soon after all. She hadn't had someone she could laugh with since she'd deserted her friends back home. Although the staff at the bar in NYC had been stellar, they weren't people she'd felt she could be her true self around. Lexi seemed to be doing a great job of seeing right through her façade; hell, Courtney couldn't remember the last time she'd felt this comfortable around another person besides Kris.

She was sitting in front of the old-fashioned mirror with her shirt pulled up when she heard the apartment door opening and closing. She'd been obsessively staring at her tattoo all morning, half in awe over it while the other half broke her heart. Seeing the memorial design carved into her flesh put things in perspective. Someone she'd loved dearly had died, and witnessing Drew's birth and death dates had her realizing she'd never forget it now. There'd been lots of times in the past year she'd woken up hoping the stabbing had only been a nightmare, that in fact Drew would be calling her any minute. Wishful thinking, that.

She saw Lexi's reflection in the mirror; she was leaning against the doorjamb, her thumbs hooked into her belt loops as she studied Courtney.

"What?"

Lexi shrugged, stepping farther in the room. "Just wondering how nobody's snatched you up yet. You must break a lot of hearts."

Courtney blinked, not expecting Lexi to say something so forward so soon. It was probably her pickup line of the day, but the comment was so bang-on, it had her looking away from Lexi. "Someone had, but yeah, I kind of fucked it up. I'm actually pretty good at that, can ruin relationships, and I don't even have to try."

Lexi reached for her hands, pulling Courtney slowly to her feet. "I take it they didn't understand the obvious restlessness inside of you?"

On the contrary; while they were together, Natalie had gone above and beyond trying to understand Courtney and all her quirks. But understanding and having to put up with it for years were two different things. The fact Courtney had no real idea if Nat had moved on since said a lot about her character. But she just nodded at Lexi, preferring not to bother with logistics. "Yeah, you could say that."

Lexi pressed a kiss to her lips, her hands resting lightly on Courtney's ass. A grin appeared. "Well, today you can forget about all that. I'm going on the assumption you've never been to Toronto, and I plan to show you all my favourite places. Starting with my favourite place to eat, 'cause I'm starving. We've gotta go out the fire escape, though; I noticed that car parked out front again."

"Fucking hell. What is that guy's problem?"

Courtney *had* been to Toronto, a few times, actually, but she chose not to divulge that to her new friend. As they left the apartment, though, bittersweet memories of Drew getting a photography award and then driving her and Mel around the city came to mind. Her best friend had been pissed at Courtney that weekend, she remembered. She'd brought the wrong guy back to their hotel room, and the bastard had stolen anything he could get his hands on, including Drew's car.

Courtney would give anything to go back in time. She'd be a better version of herself, and instead of partying with Mel, she'd insist they watch movies in the hotel room with Drew. If she could, she'd take back every single moment she and Drew had argued. She'd been young, stupid, and under the false notion they'd have all the time in the world.

She couldn't have been more wrong.

Chapter 10

"WHERE ARE YOU TAKING me?" Courtney whined, just as the frosty breeze blew the wrong way once more and another uncontrollable shudder passed through her. Fuck's sakes, she missed the milder temperatures of her hometown! At this minus thirty below shit, her nips might freeze the hell off before she and Lexi reached their destination. She briefly thought of Katie and the kids, praying they were bundled up and warm in the car or a house somewhere tonight.

"We've only walked a block, beautiful girl," Lexi commented, casting her a wry grin. Her rosy cheeks didn't have anyone fooled — she was cold too. "But I've got us a shortcut. Right this way, c'mon."

Courtney didn't see any alleys around them to cut through and was surprised when Lexi stopped in front of a set of stairs leading underground. She had to take a subway train to get to her favourite restaurant? Courtney had managed to avoid subways for twenty-three years, and the way she saw it, there was no reason to start taking them now. A taxi or an Uber would be safer, probably cleaner, and definitely faster.

"Yeah ... no. I don't do subways," Courtney blurted and then immediately wished she could call her words back. She sounded like Melanie, for god's sake. She prided herself on not being judgmental, despite her earlier paths she'd crossed with Kris before she'd gotten to know him.

Lexi just cocked her pierced eyebrow in speculation. "This isn't the subway, and you've seriously never been? That'll be a whole other experience we'll have to do together."

She was smirking, clearly trying hard not to laugh at Courtney's oddness. Even in NYC, she'd never ridden the subway, choosing to hoof it or take a bus or cab. She was aware it was irrational, considering what she'd been doing for a side job the last year. Fighting wasn't exactly a golf game in the Hamptons.

Nevertheless, Courtney took Lexi's hand, placing way more trust in the girl than she should. They'd just met, but it didn't feel like it. She couldn't explain it, but with Lexi's kindness and easygoing nature, Courtney somehow knew she was genuine. Lexi tugged her hand closer, trapping it under her arm as she led her slowly down the stairs. People bustled past them, eager to get to wherever this place led, or eager to leave it.

She was absently chewing on her bottom lip when Lexi chuckled. "You're adorable when you're worried. Besides the piss smell you're about to overload on, this place is awesome. Trust me on that. It's an underground pathway system stretching out over most of the city."

Sure enough, once they got inside the entrance Courtney got a whiff of stale coffee and urine. She had a feeling too many people passed out here and let their bladders go to town on the steps and walls. It was repulsive, to say the least, and yet as they continued onward, she got more and more impressed, along with a side dish of claustrophobia.

"You're right, it's awesome," she agreed. An underground world rested below the streets of Toronto. Well maybe not a "world" per se, but a huge mall with halls that disappeared into the distance. The place was a map, the shops and eateries located on the corners and in rows an exciting new landmark for Courtney to step foot on. Her love of shopping was coming on strong.

She grinned, pulling off her toque and mittens to stuff in her purse. "Can we shop here? What time do they close?"

"How about we come back after we eat?" Lexi suggested, patting her flat stomach over her winter bomber jacket. "I didn't have time to stop for lunch, and I'm starting to wonder what my arm would taste like."

Courtney laughed, shaking her head as they headed in one of the many directions through the mall, or whatever it was. "You sound like Kris when you talk about food. He'd like you a lot, I bet."

"Where is he now, after everything that happened?"

She shook her head, silently telling Lexi the subject was off limits. At least for now; it hurt way too much to talk about. She cleared her throat, reaching for her hand once more and enjoying the feel of her bare skin sans gloves. "Tell me about this place. I'm betting there's history here, since you seem to love it."

"You'd be on the money." Lexi stopped in front of a coffee shop, and once they were on the move again — this time with two small hot chocolates — she continued, after a few sips of her drink. "The first segment was built in 1900, a tunnel under the Eaton's on James Street. It's actually not far from where we are now, and the original pathway is still used today."

Courtney listened to her new friend explain how the network of underground pathways expanded in the 1960s, and now the entire PATH system reached thirty kilometres, making it the largest underground "mall" — as Courtney thought of it — in the world. It was obvious Lexi had a great adoration for the city she was born and raised in, not to mention her insane fascination with history. But Courtney wasn't knocking it; she too had a close relationship with obtaining knowledge and figuring out how to use it once she had it. It wasn't too long ago she'd been studying to be a teacher, of all things, and then after that she'd been taking online business classes to learn everything she could about her father's investment business.

"It's way too easy to get lost down here," Lexi was saying. She pointed at the threshold they stood on, seeming to connect one section of the tunnel to another. "See how the tile design varies? It's the only way I can remember where I'm going. Depending on which office tower block we're under, the tiles change."

"Very cool. I wonder how many people figured that out?" Courtney said before turning down another path. This strange, underground world was filled with delicious options to eat, but Lexi didn't stop until they'd exited the path system and were once again in the cold.

"Damn you, Lexi." Courtney scowled, and the lightness she'd been feeling was once again squashed by the frigid Ontario temps.

Lexi laughed, giving her a quick kiss before leading her down the street. They came upon a Canadian cuisine restaurant called Bannock, which Courtney would later realize had some of the best dishes she'd ever eaten. All too often she chose meat and salads or some other health-conscious food. She'd always been an eat-to-live girl, but damn, after sampling Bannock's infamous roast duck poutine pizza that Lexi couldn't stop raving about, she could appreciate the live to eat analogy. And the arcadian pot pie! She must have been starving or something because she ate all of hers and would have eaten more of Lexi's pizza had she not devoured it already.

The atmosphere in the restaurant was relaxing, and after they'd finished with supper, they sat back and talked over drinks. Lexi was so much more than a mere tattooist. Her personality was intricately woven, had grown and blossomed into this sexy, intellectually fun woman. Courtney was finding it harder and harder to keep her distance, slipping up to inform Lexi of the financial empire she'd fled from, and had even told her of Natalie.

"So, since you're rich and all, does that mean I should give you the bill?" Lexi wondered when they were getting ready to leave. She grinned, waving the slip of paper in her hand like she was enticing Courtney to grab it.

Courtney's face heated, already regretting she'd divulged that part of herself. "I can pay for mine, but money's tight lately. I'm not Courtney Cairns here, Lexi. I'm just Corey, a nobody, a traveller."

"You're not nobody, beautiful girl," Lexi replied, tucking the bill into the back pocket of her jeans before she snagged Courtney around the waist. She pulled her in close, her lips inches from Courtney's. "You're fire and light, beauty and brains. And so fucking hot, I wanna lift you onto this table and have you coming apart over my fingers."

Courtney sucked in a sharp breath, aware of her pulse tripping over Lexi's words of seduction, aware they weren't the only people in the restaurant and she couldn't give in to her impulses just yet. Oh, but *damn*, she had the insane urge to sink her hands into Lexi's punk-style jeans.

"You're too sexy for your own good," Courtney said, a little more breathless than she'd have liked. Fuck, she'd never had such a raging response to anyone before. Served her right for starving her sexual appetite for the past year.

"C'mon, let's get out of here." Lexi guided them to the front to pay, and before Courtney had time to prepare herself, they were outside on the sidewalk. She immediately shivered, pulling her coat closer to her neck. "Unfortunately, I lost track of time, and all the shops are probably closed by now."

Courtney held in her disappointment at that news, instead going for a smile and shrugging. "That's okay. What else can we do?"

Lexi put her arm around Courtney's shoulders, pulling her in closer as they headed down the sidewalk and to the underground PATH system once more. "I've got a few ideas."

"That involve clothes?" Courtney sniggered at the innuendo in Lexi's voice. She glanced at her. "We're friends, right? So, let's do some friends things tonight."

"Okay, beautiful girl, I got you. Although your body language is telling me otherwise, I'll ignore it. Oh, hold on a sec." Lexi let go of Courtney to pull her phone from her back pocket. She scanned what must have been a text that had come through before glancing up to Courtney again. "You like hockey?"

OH, MY FUCK, KILL me now.

Courtney looked around Chad Cole's living room an hour later, wishing she could go back in time and take Lexi up on her offer of seduction. Lexi's younger brother had his small rental jam-packed with people wearing either a Maple Leafs or Canucks jersey. Bowls and trays of snacks sat out on the coffee table, and every few minutes someone would yell at the TV. How they hadn't pissed off the downstairs neighbour yet was the question. Just about everyone had a beer in their hands, Courtney included.

She sipped hers, not loving the taste, but she'd be damned if she showed how out of place she truly was. She was neutral when it came to most sports, both hockey and football falling in that spectrum. Why she'd lied and told Lexi otherwise, she'd never know.

The seats had all been taken by the time they'd arrived, so Courtney was currently nestled between Lexi's legs and leaning her head against her chest from their position on the floor. Lexi was once again showcasing her muscle shirt, and Courtney must have spent the better part of the last hour studying her tattoo sleeves.

"Matthews is off his game tonight," Chad complained from his leather La-Z-Boy. Courtney watched him down his beer and go for another in the cooler on the floor beside him. A handful of tattoos were on display on his bicep, but nothing like his older sister. His nose had a hoop ring in the side of one nostril, and his shoulder-length black hair was pulled back with an elastic. And he had a beard that actually suited his strong cheekbones. She generally despised beards, but with Chad's fireman build, it made him look like a younger version of her old university prof — who she'd slept with, twice.

"You checkin' out my brother?"

Courtney craned her head to see Lexi gazing at her. She grinned. "Only noticing the killer genes didn't just land on you alone. He could be a model."

Lexi rolled her eyes. "Don't say that; he's got a big enough head. Eh, Chad? Corey thinks you're smokin'."

Chad sent them a shit-eating grin. "Aw, don't hate on her, Lex. It only happened the once, and you were cool with it after."

"What happened?" Courtney asked, confused. Now everyone in the room was looking in their direction, and by the sheepish glances from all their friends, it seemed she was the only one who didn't have a clue.

"I brought a girl here once before. Not even a week later, she was Chad's girl," Lexi said in a deadpan tone. She finished her beer before placing the empty can on the end table behind them.

"Prick!" Courtney exclaimed, frowning across the room at the gorgeous fucker.

"It's like, whatever. I'd dropped her anyway, so it wasn't like she was cheating." Lexi winked, running her hands over Courtney's shoulders. "Plenty of fish in the sea, beautiful girl."

"Still ... want me to beat his ass for you?" Courtney murmured moments later when the commotion of the game and its spectators had drowned out their voices.

"You're feisty, I'll give you that." Lexi dropped her face down so her lips hovered compellingly close to Courtney's. Her warm, beer-scented breath fanned Courtney's cheek seconds before she kissed her.

Courtney's eyes closed, savouring the aftertaste of the booze on Lexi's lips more than she had the actual drink. She turned in her arms, reaching up to fist one hand around her neck as she returned the kiss. She would've gladly continued the lip lock, except Lexi's girl-stealer of a brother interrupted them.

"So who's your favourite team, Corey? The Leafs or Canucks?"

Courtney reluctantly pulled away from Lexi's intoxicating air, cutting her eyes to the rest of the room before her. She met Chad's mischievous baby blues, almost identical to his sister's. "The Canucks," she lied, "but uh ... Drew MacIntyre is a good player for the Leafs." It was the only name she could come up with, and the only reason she remembered the guy's name was well, obvious. During one of their rare father-daughter trips, Sebastian had taken her to a home game against the Leafs.

A few of Chad's friends laughed at her comment, almost as if they thought she was joking. Had she gotten the name wrong? Courtney glanced back at Lexi, who just looked bored of the whole thing.

"Drew MacIntyre got traded from the Leafs in 2015," a girl in a Leafs jersey said, a bowl full of chips on her lap.

Courtney dismissed the unknown bitch with a casual wave of her hand, exuding a cockiness she didn't feel. "Like I said, Canucks are my team. The twins make the game worth watching."

Lexi groaned from behind her, and this time Chad was the one to speak up. He snorted a laugh. "The Sedin twins? They retired last season. You can't be too much of a fan."

"I've had a bit of a year." Courtney narrowed her eyes, silently daring him to argue with her. The fuck she was gonna let anyone knowingly embarrass her. She shouldn't have even bothered coming here, pretending to be someone she wasn't. She was fucking awesome without being a lover of hockey. It was a stupid sport anyway, not nearly as exciting as a bloodbath in the ring.

The game continued, and she was once again ignored, which was fine by her. She nestled against Lexi and reached for her lukewarm beer, wishing she was at a club with Melanie and downing tequila shots.

"You don't even like hockey, do you?" Lexi whispered, her lips pressing against Courtney's earlobe.

She inhaled the subtle scent she was beginning to associate with Lexi and smiled. "Not even a little." An inaudible moan left her as Lexi dragged her tongue up the side of her throat, not seeming to give a fuck who noticed their PDA.

"Wanna bounce?"

Courtney felt dazed when she opened her eyes, and she nodded, half out of it with need. "Fuck, yes."

"DREW, STOP!"

I'm calling her name, but my voice seems to carry away in the crowd. My heart is spazzing out, and I can't figure out why my best friend is running toward Dobie. She should be hauling ass away from the little psycho!

"Drew, stop! Wait!" I scream. I'm running too but hoping I can get to her before she does something utterly stupid.

"No!!!" I'm screeching as I see Drew get stabbed. What the fuck is happening? The crowd is going nuts, and Drew is fighting back like a knife didn't just get yanked from her chest.

I'm frozen in place, as if I know what's coming at the end of a horror flick. I'm already screaming when the hunting knife sinks into her flesh again and again. I'm crying out her name as her shirt stains red.

"Baby girl, no. Please not her. Anyone but her. Any fucking body!!"

Courtney woke with a start, immediately aware of the clammy sweat on her forehead and between her breasts. It took several attempts to settle her racing pulse, even more to rid her mind of Drew's body being used as a butcher block.

She wasn't disoriented; she knew she was still in Lexi's bed. For a moment or two she even burrowed deeper into her sleeping arms, desperate to be comforted; that is, until she got her wits back.

She couldn't ... *refused* to rely on anyone to be her shelter. *She* was her shelter, just as she'd been for the past year; fuck, for her entire life it seemed most days. No one could give her mind and body what it needed better than she, even if sometimes she denied it. Her brain craved the love and connection it'd been lacking since Drew died, and now her body craved Lexis's warmth, her sensual passion and zest for life.

It was a trap.

She'd been down this road before. Falling for someone, letting them in just enough that it hurt when shit went a-tumbling. There was no goddamn way she'd ever let such a disaster happen again. Honestly, the reason she felt vulnerable now was most likely because she hadn't fought since January. Finding balance was crucial in her life.

Courtney carefully lifted Lexi's arm currently draped across her midsection, high enough that she was able to slide out of her tempting embrace and off the bed. She put on her glasses before checking the glowing clock on the alarm sitting on the nightstand behind Lexi's head. It wasn't even half past three in the morning — way too early to sneak out into a city she wasn't used to. And besides, she wasn't the same girl she'd been a year ago. As much as her instincts said otherwise, she wouldn't run from Lexi. They weren't a couple, so she didn't owe her any promises for the future. She'd say her goodbyes like the mature adult she was. To her face, with a smile. Besides, she'd managed to secure a Workaway placement in Montreal for the month of April and May, so she would've left sooner or later. It made sense to leave now; the last thing she could possibly deal with right now was falling for someone new.

She left Lexi to sleep, instead pulling on her sports bra and black tights. She grabbed her scrunchie from the side pocket of her duffel bag and twisted her auburn curls into a messy ponytail. Then she carried her socks and sneakers quietly out of the bedroom, shutting the door silently behind her. She helped herself to a drink of water from the kitchen sink before she got her footwear on, not wasting any time jumping into a squat routine. She'd began following a YouTube trainer when she realized she wouldn't be able to train with her kick boxing instructor if she was on the road. So, she'd started calisthenic workouts she was able to do using just her body, and the results had been huge. Her ass was full of sass and shape now and her legs strong for kicking the crap out of her opponents, but it was her abs she loved the best. Her hard work showed in the sexy indents on her tummy, and the strength in her now could take a good beating in the ring, as much as the next fighter.

Damn, she missed fighting!

Arching up to her tiptoes from her squat position had the back of her legs stretching nicely. She did those for forty-five seconds and then promptly fell into alternating stationary lunges. She kept her hands on her hips as she lunged, dipping low and keeping watch where her knee placement was. Her pulse was picking up, but this time it was from the adrenaline in her workout, not from a nightmare. Her hair was damp with perspiration by the time she reached the seated in and outs, but damned if she wasn't feeling better. She now understood the pull exercise could have on a person, maybe even why Drew had always felt she needed to swim for hours. The difference was, her bestie had used it to punish herself for so long that her body could never tell what was or wasn't healthy.

Everything in life needed a balance, it turned out.

Focusing on the outlandish painting on the wall in the hallway, she drew in her knees to her chest and then stretched her legs out once more, making sure to keep them off the floor and her tummy tight. She had already started on her push-ups when she heard the door to Lexi's bedroom open.

Courtney watched her stumble her way to the bathroom, still half asleep. She heard the toilet flush a minute later, and then the tap water run. She pushed up again, then down, feeling every muscle in her arm stretch with the movement.

"Courtney? You okay?" Lexi drowsily called. "Oh, shit. And I mean that ... positively. Positively shit, you're *gorgeous* right now, beautiful girl."

Courtney felt Lexi's wandering gaze on her as she lowered herself into the last two pushups in the rep. She knew exactly what she looked like hot and sweaty from a workout, and how Lex thought she was gorgeous she couldn't fathom. Her cheeks were flushed red with exertion, her glasses a bit fogged from the heat, her scalp dripping with sweat, and the rest of her was ... well, moist all over.

She laughed; it was a nice release compared with the misery she'd felt a half hour or so ago when she'd woken after the nightmare. "You're half asleep and clearly blind."

Shifting into a sitting position, Courtney started her cool-down routine with some basic stretches. The stretching was just as important to her as the workout. She'd lost count how many hamstrings she'd pulled from not stretching afterward. She'd gotten through five minutes with Lexi's smouldering gaze on her before she couldn't take it anymore and called it quits. She had a strong feeling her workout wasn't finished just yet.

"See something you want?" Courtney teased as she breezed past Lexi to the bathroom. She bent over the clawfoot tub to plug the drain before she turned the taps on. It was still way too early for a bath, but she'd used Lexi's shower the morning before and didn't really like it. She'd had to pull the curtain all around the tub, and she'd felt like one of those victims in a horror movie where the killer attacks them in the shower and suffocates them with the curtain. What movie was that scene in, *Psycho*? Even if it was just a movie, she had no doubt crazies like that existed in the world.

Lexi entered the bathroom, clearly taking the open door as an invitation. "I don't think I've ever seen anyone do a pushup like that."

Courtney glanced over her shoulder at her. Having just come from bed, Lexi looked softer, younger than her thirty-one, especially with the men's tight white tank top on and women's Woxer briefs. And she always seemed ready for sex, like nothing else in life would bother her enough not to want sex.

Huh. Now that Courtney thought about it, she'd just described herself to some degree.

"There's quite a few ways to do a pushup," she informed her, turning back to the water and checking the temperature. She increased the hot water more and wasn't at all surprised when Lexi placed a hand on her bare back.

"Your tattoo looks good." Her curious fingers were making their way around Courtney's torso as she stood up.

Courtney brushed past her to the sink, eager to get her contacts in. There was nothing worse than having sex and everything being blurry.

"No, hey. Leave them on," Lexi said from behind. She reached for Courtney's hand, turning her gently to catch the mischief in her blue eyes. "I've got a whole teacher fantasy running around my head right now. Or maybe a scientist. A sexy scientist working on something top-secret for the government."

"Fuck you." But Courtney couldn't help but grin. How could she say no to those eyes and eager hands? She was still wearing her glasses when Lexi stripped her of her workout tights and then impatiently helped Courtney with her sports bra. Before she knew it, she was twisted around again and bent over facing the bathroom sink mirror.

"No, beautiful girl. Fuck *you*. And hell, yes I plan to. And so very *well*."

She let out a soft cry when Lexi pulled her ponytail, but it was a cry of intense pleasure rippling through her. She could hear her breaths coming out desperately as she met Lexi's eyes in the mirror. She swallowed before clasping her hand over the one Lexi had gripping her hip. "No, Lexi Cole. This time I'm taking full control."

Her two years of either sparring or fighting had her moving faster then Lexi could grasp. Courtney had her small frame lifted onto the bathroom counter in seconds and, spotting the rope they'd used the night before near the soap dish, she quickly tied it to one wrist.

"Don't forget the tub's still running," Lexi murmured, watching with interest as Courtney secured both wrists to the towel holder. With her arms above her head and locked in place, her small breasts jutted out in front of Courtney. Lexi was still half dressed in her underthings, but Courtney made quick work of that as well. Spotting her camo pants on the floor a few feet away, she rifled through the pockets until she came out with the pocketknife she always carried.

"Regret tying me up already? Payback's a bitch," Lexi said with a sly smile. She was having fun with this.

Courtney bit her lip, flicking the small knife open and silently reaching for Lexi's tank top. She heard a slight hitch in Lexi's breath as she began cutting the shirt right down the middle. Four or five tugs of the blade later, Lexi's tank top had become an erotic, seam-torn shirt vest. Seriously, Courtney should've gone to fashion school.

"Better," she said with a flash in her eyes as she caught sight of Lexi's hardened peaks now on display. She pointed to her Woxers. "Those are a problem, though."

"Courtney, you're killing me here." Lexi groaned, thrusting her hips out instinctively at Courtney's attention. She was close to falling off the countertop.

"Careful there. Don't fall and ruin this for me," Courtney warned. She ran her tongue over her bottom lip, already imagining what she wanted to do to

Lexi. She reached for the hem of the Woxers and slowly cut a v out of the material, just large enough to expose all of Lexi's beauty.

"And you think I'm gorgeous," she said with an incredulous shake of her head. She leaned into Lexi long enough to nip her chin. Lexi moved in to kiss her, but Courtney pulled away, wagging her finger.

"Where are you going?"

Courtney crossed over to the clawfoot tub and shut off the taps. Then she had an idea, and she gleefully ran with it.

"Beautiful girl, what are you doing to me? You're not gonna leave me like this?" Lexi demanded, watching as Courtney tested the water with one foot.

She turned back to Lexi with a laugh, watching as she rattled the ropes back and forth on the towel holder. Courtney hadn't tied them very tight and knew Lexi could get out of them if she truly wanted to.

"I don't want the water to go to waste," she replied, shimmying out of her bikini briefs. She tested the water again, deciding she could handle it, and slowly lifted into the tub. It was a bit scalding at first, but her body soon adjusted. Her nipples strained to an unbearable tightness under Lexi's intense gaze, and for a second she thought of cutting the ropes so they could bathe together. But they weren't a couple, and sharing a bath was something she used to do with Natalie.

"I don't need prepping, if that's what you're worried about," Lexi grunted, and then a low moan escaped her when Courtney began squirting her masculine body wash over her breasts. "I'm more than ready, beautiful girl. If you don't believe me, come have a taste."

"I'm not worried. I'm sweaty, and so I'm washing myself," Courtney insisted, sounding all too playful. Torturing Lexi was turning out sweeter than she'd imagined. Who knew the dom could play the sub when they wanted to?

She continued to lather herself with soap, after a while reaching for a washcloth out of the decorative basket near the tub. In her rush to seduce, she'd forgotten to wash her hair first and briefly wondered how awful it'd be if she rinsed her hair in the soapy water. Aware Lexi still had her blue gaze trained on her every move, Courtney grabbed the shower nozzle instead and prayed the tub wouldn't overfill.

"Your hair is fucking sexy. I love when it's around me, touching me," Lexi choked out as Courtney massaged shampoo into her scalp. She looked so turned on, Courtney almost felt bad for her. But it would just make the result sooo much more exquisite.

"Hmm, too bad you'll have to wait, lover," she crooned a moment later, arching her back and tilting her face up to rinse out the shampoo. By the time she was stepping out of the tub, Lexi was doing her own amount of sweating. She was straining against the rope, looking like she might very well break the restraints.

Courtney unhurriedly closed the distance between them, not in any haste to forfeit the sexual power she currently had on her tattooist. When there were mere inches keeping them apart, she used the bath towel in her hands to dry herself in deliberate, languid strokes.

A surprised gasp escaped Lexi, seconds before she sucked her lip between her teeth and let her head fall to the side. Her thighs were trembling, and the ragged exhales coming from her had Courtney dropping her towel to cup Lexi's cheek. She couldn't stop the grin forming as she placed kisses along her jawline.

"First time I ever made a girl orgasm without touching them."

"What can I say?" Lexi mumbled, peering up at her in question, like she was trying to figure out how Courtney did it. She swallowed. "I really love women. The shape of your body is ... fuck, beautiful girl."

Lexi groaned, her eyelids fluttering closed again as Courtney kissed a path down her body, slipping off the cut up shirt far enough to kiss her shoulders and collarbone.

"Cut me loose now. My arms are asleep and killing me."

Courtney considered the request as she ran her tongue up one side of Lexi's breast, closing her hands on the small mounds to give them a firm squeeze. If she cut Lexi loose, she had a feeling she'd lose any control she had. Was she okay with that?

She'd have to be. Whether or not Lexi was bluffing, it felt wrong to continue after she'd been told to stop with the rope. So Courtney straightened up to kiss her lips, at the same time reaching for the pocketknife she'd left on the counter. And sure enough, as soon as she was free Lexi grabbed her under the armpits and pulled her to the bathroom floor.

"I'm leaving today," Courtney blurted, needing to get the admission off her chest.

Lexi looked temporarily sidelined, but then she was straddling Courtney and pulling off her torn tank top. Seriously, nothing could dampen her mood enough that she wouldn't want sex, and Courtney kind of admired her for it.

"Like I said before, beautiful girl," Lexi whispered and wasted zero time burying her tattooed fingers between Courtney's legs. A loud moan left her as her eyes momentarily rolled back in her head at the feel of Lexi's persistent movement. She was still half blind with desire when Lexi devoured her mouth, bruising her with her kiss. Courtney loved it, though — craved the intensity and made sure she wasn't just going along for the ride. She had her hands on Lexi's back, ready to sink her nails in when everything came to a halt; everything, her approaching orgasm included.

Courtney growled in frustration when she realized the ploy Lexi was using. Before she'd been all over Courtney, so much they'd been sharing one breath, and now? Lexi sat back on her hunches with a clandestine grin.

"What the fuck, Lex?"

Lexi reached for one of Courtney's feet, lifting the leg up to place a kiss on her arch. She chuckled. "Like I said before. Payback's a bitch, beautiful girl."

Chapter 11

Montreal, QC, April 9

"FUCK!" COURTNEY GROWLED, STUMBLING backward and watching in slow motion as her opponent's fist barrelled into her face again. Now she knew why the dark-skinned woman was nicknamed Speed Smack — 'cause she flew at Courtney so fast, she could barely register the blow. She circled the ring with her opponent, her fists shielding her face and her elbows blocking her ribs. It was a chilly night in Montreal, and yet she could feel perspiration trickling down through her sports bra. She spat out the blood oozing around her tongue, narrowly sidestepping another punch and managing to get in one of her own. Her right eye was already closing over, so her perception was slightly off when she kicked Speed Smack; she'd been aiming for her stomach, but the blow landed half-assed across her thigh instead. It threw off her balance, and quicker than she could blink, Speed Smack had one arm around Courtney's hip and the other fist pounding into her kidney.

She couldn't be certain, but it felt as if Speed Smack was legitimately trying to *kill* her. At the rate she was jumbling her insides, Courtney would be pissing blood for a week.

Fuck this. Fuck it all the way to Sunday and back.

Courtney fisted her hands into Speed Smack's shoulders, digging her nails in as much as they would go — which wasn't much, since she never let them grow out anymore, and with a swift jerk she spun the bitch around like a top toy. Speed Smack stumbled away from her, and Courtney made sure she didn't waste the upper hand she was given. Grounding her weight to the concrete beneath her, she swung into a turning kick and rammed her foot exactly where she aimed it.

Speed Smack instinctively clutched her stomach in pain, and that was all the invitation Courtney needed. Lifting her leg again, she side-kicked her hard in the ribs, and when her opponent faltered, Courtney slammed a left hook into her unprotected face followed by a brutal right uppercut. Speed Smack swayed before dropping down on one knee.

Courtney could barely see, but hell's bells, she was riding on a sudden burst of adrenaline. The cheering crowd faded, and all she could process was how to put an end to the bitch before her. She kicked her in the face, and the moment Speed Smack fell, Courtney attacked her opponent like a vicious dog; except instead of biting, she had her fists flying as she straddled her on the ground.

It wasn't until the referee dragged Courtney off a moment later that she realized she'd won and the other girl was unconscious. He held her hand up, showing her off to the hollering spectators, and Courtney didn't wait around for Speed Smack to wake up. She was ready to collapse herself, and she'd rather not do it here. So she collected her prize after grabbing her belongings and was headed toward the exit when she heard footsteps running up behind her.

"Well, now I know why you call yourself Corey. This alter ego is whacked compared to regular Courtney."

Courtney turned stiffly around, wincing through the eye that hadn't completely swollen shut yet. Joy encompassed her when she saw who was standing there, but it quickly turned to an exhausted annoyance. "Lexi, what are you doing in Montreal?" Not that she wasn't happy to see her, because she was, but Courtney was no damsel in distress. The worry in Lexi's eyes made it crystal-clear she wanted to be Courtney's knight.

But she just grinned, her tattooed arm coming out to loop through Courtney's. "I spontaneously flew here, deciding I had to see you fight for myself. I'll admit, it was both hot and horrifying for me."

Courtney came to a stop, guiltily pulling her arm away from her friend's. "I appreciate your help getting me into the fight, and I think the world of you, but you shouldn't have come. I'm not — not in a good frame of mind."

"I realized that when you went to town on the other girl. She might need plastic surgery after tonight; hell, you might need it too. How can you even see?"

"Barely," Courtney muttered, continuing out to the parking lot.

They had bypassed security before Lexi spoke again. "I checked into a hotel for the night. Come back with me, Courtney. I'll pamper the shit out of you."

"I'm serious, Lexi. I'll be fine on my own." She tripped on the curb of the sidewalk she was hell-bent on walking down. Her current place of residence was down this way somewhere. Her head was throbbing so hard that in a daze she wondered if Speed Smack had given her a damn concussion.

"You need me, at least for tonight. It's not wrong for someone to take care of you every now and then," Lexi insisted, grabbing her arm again when she tripped a second time. Her vision was ... hell, what vision? She had shit-all at the moment. She'd never been struck in the face so much at one time.

"I've been beaten up before, with no one around. I took care of myself."

Lexi wrapped Courtney's arm around her shoulder, holding on to her waist and guiding her down the street. "I bet you said that about a lot of things growing up, beautiful girl."

Courtney felt her elephant-sized head tip over to rest on Lexi's. She was so sore and tired, she could probably sleep for the next three days. Her boarding hosts would be pissed, though, if she didn't earn her keep while staying there for free. There would be bed linens to strip and wash and grocery runs to make for their café. She groaned. "I need to get back to the B&B."

A kiss landed against her hairline. "What you need is to soak in a hot bubble bath while you ice your eyes. I'll grab their digits off you and give them a buzz while you rest. You definitely don't wanna be going back there looking like roadkill."

Lexi had a point, and besides, it wasn't like she'd be much good cleaning house in the state she was in.

"You sure know how to talk to the ladies, Lexi."

Chapter 12

"I THINK YOU'VE GOT a concussion."

Courtney groaned at her badgering, wishing she could at least open one eye to glare. The ice pack started to slip, so she reached out from under the hot bath water to reposition it. "I'll be fine."

She heard Lexi shuffle over to the Jacuzzi tub. Courtney could smell her masculine body spray, she was so close; it nearly drove her crazy not being able to see what was going on around her. She jumped a little when Lexi's hands started unravelling her braid, and she winced from what the pulling and tugging was doing to her scalp.

"The crazy bitch Speed whatever got you pretty good here," Lexi said, quietly and lightly pressing on an area above Courtney's temple. "Between me and you, I think her name is a concoction of what she must be taking before her fights. 'Cause you'd have to be fucking high to move so fast."

Courtney sucked in a sharp breath, her hand soaring up to halt Lexi's concerned invasion. "Careful; some of the blood is matted in my hair."

"I know. I'm gonna wash it." Sure enough, a moment later the nozzle spray was turned on and Lexi was easing Courtney's head back against the tub rest. She sighed as her friend slowly allowed the water to caress her beaten-up head.

"I'm glad you're here," she murmured, albeit reluctantly. She didn't *want* to need Lexi; she'd been doing fine on her own. She couldn't even fathom what might've happened had she been strolling around downtown Montreal like this by herself.

"I'm worried about you, beautiful girl. Have you given any thought to what an injury could do to your gorgeous eyes? Fuck, somebody hit you hard enough, you could go blind."

"I hope you're not falling for me, Lexi Cole. Friends only, remember?"

Lexi's hands paused massaging shampoo into Courtney's mass of wet curls. "This is the friend in me talking, dumbass. I care about my friends, and you, Courtney, you're playing a very dangerous game in those underground fights. My cousin lost at least one buddy from doing that. He got knocked out and then had a brain bleed. Never woke up."

"Hey, you're the one who got me in touch with the right people," Courtney replied, wishing she could see her now. She removed the defrosting bag of ice from her eyes and was pleasantly surprised when she could slit one eyelid open. The satisfaction quickly fled when the light in the room made her head spin. Her stomach rolled as invisible daggers stabbed into her skull. Between that and her relentless headache, she was confident she had a concussion, as Lexi predicted.

How could she explain to Lexi the reason she fought was because when she was in physical agony, her emotional shit got benched for a day or two? Such a line of reasoning sounded masochistic, but it was the truth.

"You didn't tell me your Workaway hosts only spoke French. Neither one of us understood the other, so I hung up," Lexi said, rinsing her hair now. She really was a true friend; Courtney had come to realize that over the last month. They'd stayed in touch over texting and Facebook as Courtney roamed the cities, trying to feel out where she belonged.

By the time Lexi was finished with her hair, Courtney was shivering and certain it had nothing to do with the water temperature and everything to do with the concussion. Lexi insisted on helping her out of the tub, and when her feet touched the mat on the floor, her legs wobbled. "Whoa."

"Easy there," Lexi said, covering her with a towel. Like she did outside the warehouse, she wrapped one arm around Courtney's lean waist, carefully guiding her to the hotel bed. She felt the mattress press against her bare leg a moment later.

"I think the concussion is only mild, so as long as I take it easy, I should be fine," she mumbled, exhaustion taking over. Shit, and she hadn't had the opportunity for her post-fight celebration drink yet.

"I'm starting to hate that fucking word. Everything is fine with you. How about you tell me something real and not just fine?" Irritation rolled off Lexi as she helped Courtney slip into bed. She took her time resting her battered head onto the white pillows and wondered if blood would be all over them come morning.

She heard Lexi pulling off her leathers and jacket, and then she was slipping under the covers behind Courtney. "I was in love with Drew for years," she whispered, not even sure Lexi could hear her. That was okay, though; she was saying it for herself. "I wasted years hiding my feelings, and when she finally found out, I ran. She didn't love me like that, was already pregnant with Kris's kid and crazy in love. So, then I went a month or more avoiding her, not knowing what to say or do, and as time went on thinking I wasn't in love with her like I thought I was."

"You couldn't have known what would happen."

Silence stretched out between them. At one point, Lexi pulled on a bathrobe and went to get more ice down the hall. She filled up the bags again, and Courtney felt the cool towel cover her eyes once more.

"You want real, and so I'll give it to you," Courtney finally continued, emptiness creeping into her tone now. She swallowed. "I'm not over her or her death. I want to *kill* the piece of shit who murdered her. I wanna kill her fiancé who was also my friend, and sometimes I wanna kill myself. Fighting keeps all of it in check, Lexi, and the pain makes me hurt less."

"I'm sorry, Courtney." Lexi's hand splayed comfortingly across the blanket covering her bare tummy. "Drew must have been really special."

Tears pricked her eyelids. A part of her hated that Lexi was tearing down walls around her frozen heart. She hadn't spoken the painful truth to anyone, not even Natalie. "She was; you would've fallen for her too."

"What was she like?"

Courtney shook her head, and the stabbing pain that followed made her stomach lurch in protest. "No more, please. It's too hard, and I'm tired."

"No worries, beautiful girl. I'll be here for you whenever you wanna open up."

Never; she never wanted to open up. Rehashing all the wonderful memories she'd made with Drew and her family over the years cut her to the fucking bone. The agony that she'd never again have that familial sense of belonging broke her heart. Speaking of the happier times just made her more depressed. No, it was easier this way — just to shove it down as fervently as possible.

She fell asleep sometime after, even without the aid of her nightly routine of sobbing through old pictures. Lexi had been curled up beside her, and when Courtney woke hours later drenched in sweat from her nightmare, she sought solace.

Lexi woke easily when Courtney reached for her in the dark. Her eyelids were still swollen and her throbbing headache present, and she could scarcely make out Lexi's questioning gaze. "I need you to fuck me, Lex. I–I'm too wound up, and my mind is crazy right now. I need you to take me away from it all."

The sharp inhale from Lexi said she was down for sex, but when she threw the bed sheets aside and straddled Courtney, she paused. "Are you sure? You're beat all to hell, Courtney. I don't wanna break you."

"You could never, but just in case, don't kiss me too rough. I might've loosened a tooth."

Lexi groaned, clearly not liking the sound of that. Courtney closed her eyes as Lexi very gently moved her lips over hers. Her mouth had been bleeding quite a bit during the fight with Speed Smack, but besides a small cut on her upper lip and having bit her tongue hard, she'd come away unscathed in that region. "There's been others since you," Lexi said, pulling back from her lips to trail her tongue down Courtney's throat.

Pleasure shot through Courtney's pussy, and she lifted her stiff legs to wrap around Lexi's hips. Her arm went around her shoulders, fingers sinking into her thick locks. "Good; I wouldn't want it any other way." She guided Lexi's kisses back to her lips, opening her mouth as Lexi's tongue swept over hers. A soft whimper escaped Courtney as her piercing dragged across the tender spot where she'd bitten her tongue in the fight. Instead of pulling back, Courtney pushed past the discomfort and met Lexi stroke for stroke. Passion shook her, and as she reached for the hem of Lexi's Woxers, her fingers were trembling in need. She hadn't been with anyone since Lexi, and the desperate way she was yanking her underwear off was a sure sign she'd been suffering without.

Lexi broke away with a devious chuckle, scattering her lips and tongue along Courtney's neck. She stopped at her ear, whispering hotly, "I see you've been fasting again."

Courtney grinned, finally satisfied when Lexi raised up long enough to shake her legs free of the undergarment and remove her tank top. Then they were skin on skin, the slick opening between Lexi's legs intimately kissing Courtney's delicate folds. She was breathing hard, seemingly unable to catch her breath, and she reached down to part her lips, bucking her hips to feel her clit stroke Lexi. The euphoric sensation of them fucking like that didn't last, however, as moments later Lexi slid down her body to cup her breasts. The hard pebbles strained under Lexi's thumbs, eager as hell for her lips and tongue. When she kissed her everywhere but there, Courtney let out a frustrated curse.

"You're a torturous bitch, Lexi Cole," she carped, making certain to tease her just as much. Courtney skimmed her fingers up the inside of Lexi's thighs, her thumb teasing the opening. She let it slip in between Lexi's folds and then back out, all the while running her fingers up and down her labia. Courtney's hand was soaked already, telling her Lexi was as invested in this as she was.

"Now who's torturing?" Lexi asked, making a point of rocking her hips against Courtney's hand. Her pierced tongue darted out, finally circling Courtney's sensitive peaks, one and then the other. She closed her mouth over Courtney's breast, sucking her nipple hard and then letting it pop out.

Courtney groaned, giving into the pleasure being offered. She raked her free hand down Lexi's back, flexing her nails into her skin. She brushed her other hand past Lexi's folds, her thumb quickly locating her clit. Her first two fingers sank in as far as they would go, and Lexi froze, temporarily pausing her attention on Courtney's breasts. She could hear Lexi's elevated breaths, felt the hot air panting so close to her nipple, and the faster she pumped her fingers, the faster those pants came.

Lexi returned her attention to Courtney's breasts and then dipped her fingers inside Courtney, who shook her head and then was momentarily dizzy from the movement. Sweat was already trickling down the side of her face. "I wanna taste you."

Seeming to know exactly what she meant, Lexi lowered her face to Courtney's for another hot kiss before turning to backwards-straddle her. When her ass appeared in Courtney's line of sight seconds later, she didn't waste time grabbing Lexi's hips to guide her entrance to Courtney's mouth. She found a rhythm with Lexi, lapping with their tongues and pumping their fingers. Courtney found her g-spot easily, making sure to drag her fingers over the sensitive area with each stroke. Lexi came first, moaning as she drenched Courtney's fingers and lips. She kept working her until the orgasm had passed, and then Lexi was crawling down Courtney's body, hot in pursuit.

Courtney laughed, but it ended with a gasp as Lexi spread her thighs wide and dove back in. Her tongue was doing wonders in both relaxing and tensing Courtney, but it wasn't until she started fucking her hard with her fingers that Courtney exploded.

It was a long time before Courtney's pulse slowed enough to speak. Her breath was airy as she said in the dim of the room, "Fuck, Lexi, you just keep setting the bar higher. How am I ... going to find anyone better in bed?"

Lexi gave a soft laugh, sidling up next to her. Courtney turned onto her side, and she didn't even need to ask. Lexi just wrapped her in her arms, silently spooning her. "I was about to say the same thing," she murmured. "It was hard settling when I knew you were out there."

"You just wait until I'm healed up. I'll turn your body into my own personal workout regime."

"God, I hope so."

Courtney smiled, snuggling deeper into Lexi's arms. She was drowsy, the constant headache making her temples throb, and her eyelids were still battered, but damn, she felt good. She was sated for the time being.

"*Now* I'll be able to fall asleep."

Chapter 13

Avenue Argyle, Montréal

COURTNEY STARED AT THE face filling up her computer screen, a turbulent mix of reactions passing through her fuddled mind and into her heart. Guilt was present — of course it was — but also a huge, unsuspecting dose of heartache she could've done without. Her right index finger hovered over the mouse, knowing she should keep scrolling, but something held her rooted in place and staring at Natalie's image. Her ex had her arms around another girl in an affectionate lip-lock, some sandy-haired bimbo with breasts the size of Dolly Parton's. The fuck she was gay, Courtney wanted to argue, but living in Vancouver as Natalie was now, anything went, including fake tits on lesbians. Anger was definitely present within Courtney, but she couldn't decipher if she was pissed at Natalie for moving on or with herself for letting such a gem go in the first fucking place.

Fuck, she was terrible with relationships.

A massive lump lodged halfway down her throat, accompanying the sting of tears behind her battered eyes as she glared at Natalie's updated relationship status. In a relationship — officially — with said bimbo, Lisa who-the-fuck-cares Lonergan. *Bitch.*

An IM popped up on her screen, and Courtney debated answering it or not. She'd been hardcore avoiding old ties this past year, and she wasn't sure she was ready to bring them back into the fold. Even as she was thinking it'd be better if she avoided Melanie a little longer, she found herself clicking on the message from Drew's twin.

Hey! Omg, you're online! How are you Court are you ok???

Courtney closed her eyes, taking a brief pause to massage her temples. Her concussion was still prevalent, and she knew she'd be forced from the desktop soon. The screen increased the pressure behind her eyes tenfold, to a point of nausea, vomiting, and insane migraines. She'd discovered that the last time she was concussed after a fight.

Deciding not to get too comfortable with her choice of words, Courtney typed back, *Fine. Safe, hbu?*

A sad face emoji appeared, and then the screen indicated Melanie was typing a message. *I'm good. We've all been worried about you. I got a record deal and am singing now. I'll be headlining a concert in Toronto next month! Super pumped. Maybe you could be there?? Where are you these days?? When are you coming home? Drew wasn't the only one who loved you, you know.*

Courtney's stomach tightened with the massive info dump just dropped in her lap. Melanie was a singer now? Man, life had a funny way of turning out. Her friend had sworn she'd never professionally sing, convinced they were all greedy, deceiving bastards in the music industry. Drew leaving them had impacted everyone so differently. They were doing things she'd never thought they'd do. Except for Kris; Courtney had known the instant she'd met him that he wasn't a hundred percent mentally. The fact that he blatantly told her he and Drew were just friends — and *believed* it as truth — had had her alarms going off. What a fucking idiot Kris was back then. You didn't become friends with Drew Matheson and *not* fall in love with her. She should know, and really, should have warned him away a hell of a lot more forcibly than she had. A sassy verbal lashing hadn't been nearly enough threat to keep their future fallout from happening. No, if Courtney could go back in time to that night at the pub, she'd have gone full-throttle on Kris's ass.

Courtney blinked, aware she'd been dazed. Another symptom of her concussed brain. She stared bleary-eyed at Melanie's message, deciding to end their convo with a mere two-liner. *Congrats. I'm currently in Montreal, for how long I can't say. Much love to you and your beautiful family. I miss you.*

She hadn't meant to put the last part, but her traitorous mind must have had other plans. The pain in her head was beginning to thump like a stereo's bass, so she backed out of the message with Melanie. She was pushing the mouse arrow up to log off when another IM popped up, and she accidently clicked on it.

"Shit," she muttered, and just like a lying, cheating teenaged girl, her heart immediately sped up to match her sweaty palms as guilt and remorse overtook her at Natalie's words.

I know you're online, and honestly, I give up trying to reach you. I just hope you're okay, and you're out in the world finding whatever it is you need to find. I'm over what did or didn't happen with us, and I even get why you felt you couldn't open up to me. Sometimes it takes losing someone to truly find yourself, and I really hope that's what you're doing. For what it's worth, I'm terribly sorry about Drew. I have my own regrets, mainly over wasting so much time being jealous when I should've been trying to get to know her.

A stupid, tiny part of me might always love you, Courtney, but don't ever come home thinking you'll win me over a third time. I've moved on, I'm sorry. It never was the right time for us. Take care of yourself.

Courtney had barely logged off Facebook before she was expelling sharp exhales through her nostrils as she tried to calm herself. Several areas hurt at once, but the gut-wrenching pang she was experiencing caused her to bend over and grip her sides like she was expecting something to fall out. The sorrow was fucking real, completely throwing her off-guard, and for a moment she didn't dare to blink. The tears were on the brink of flooding her cheeks, and she refused to go there.

Natalie had told her something the first time she'd broken off their engagement. She'd said Courtney couldn't truly love two people at once, so if she loved Drew like Natalie was accusing, then being with Natalie was a waste of time. Then they'd sorted out the mess, and Courtney had been convinced she'd been in love with only Natalie ... until Drew died. God, what a screwed-up situation it all was, but Courtney knew to her very core that she'd loved both women.

To *hell* with the past tense.

She *still* loved both women. She didn't know what she'd expected of Natalie, but up and washing her hands of Courtney hadn't been it.

There was a knock on the door, obtusely yanking her from her painful thoughts. Courtney glanced over to see her Workaway host just in the threshold of the computer room. "Je savais que tu étais pire que ce que tu voulais dire!"

"I knew you were worse than you were letting on!"

Courtney shook her head and regretted it right after. She grimaced, silently guessing at what war her body was waging, because it was a toss between bawling like a baby or puking up the butternut squash soup she'd had for supper. She straightened, making a point to push in her chair and paste on a smile for Jaclyn's benefit. She replied in French as well, *"I'm fine, honestly. I'll be ready to work in the morning, and again, I'm sorry I was out so long today."*

Jaclyn waved her hand, effectively dismissing Courtney's apology. She and her husband were both in their thirties and could barely speak a word of English, and yet they owned a bed and breakfast right in the city. They made it work, offering refuge to travellers who worked and translated for them in exchange for food, shelter, and weekends off to tour the city. A pretty sweet deal on Courtney's part, as long as she didn't screw it up. She spoke five languages, after all, and hadn't used half of them in way too long.

"If your headache isn't better by tomorrow, I want to take you to the hospital. Your fall down the stairs could have hurt more than you know."

Courtney grimaced, wishing she hadn't felt the need to lie about the cause of her injuries. Problem was, the sort of fighting she did was all kinds of illegal, and she'd rather not put such pressure on anyone. Besides, with the cut-off gloves Courtney wore all the time now, Jaclyn had never seen the state of her hands, so she was none the wiser.

Since she knew she'd never win this argument without raising serious eyebrows and ten more questions, she politely agreed. Jaclyn smiled, relief washing over her that Courtney seemed to be listening to reason. She was pretty, quite slender with medium-length brown tendrils and bangs that perfectly suited her. She had warm brown eyes, and she and her husband Maurice had been nothing but kind to Courtney in the last couple of weeks. She'd do well to remember not everyone was out to get her. Not like the mysterious man who'd been tailing her, anyway. She'd somehow managed to shake him since Toronto; she was unsure if he'd lost her or given up, but she finally felt she wasn't being followed.

"Bonne nuit," Courtney said, trying and failing this time at a smile. Who could fake smile when the woman they apparently still deeply cared for had moved on and left them behind? She realized she'd been the one to disappear, but Natalie was the therapist, not her. Couldn't she have been more patient with Courtney?

"Bonne nuit, Corey," Jaclyn returned, stepping aside to let Courtney past.

When she was safely tucked away in her private bedroom, Courtney washed up in the attached bathroom. She took notice of the heavily bruised skin around her eyes. She looked like a fucking raccoon, and the idea Lexi had exhausted her from sex all day in her damaged state was comical. She washed her face, going gently around her eyes, and then removed her contacts. Her dark blue rectangular glasses hid the bruises quite a bit, but not as much as the sunglasses Lexi had picked up would for the next few days. Cleaning the five bedrooms of the bed and breakfast would mean she'd be possibly interacting with clientele; explaining the damage thirty thousand times wasn't her cup of tea. Best to avoid it at all costs.

When she was finished and dressed in her favourite silk pajamas she'd taken with her from Vancouver, she crawled under the sheets and put her glasses on the nightstand with her cup of water. She shimmied until her back was halfway on the two pillows, resting on the otherwise vacant side of the bed. Then she grabbed her teddy to hold close to her before tucking the thick quilt in around her. When she was satisfied she was comfortable, she reached for the old cell under her pillow.

AS IT TURNED OUT, the sunglasses only helped about fifty percent. The other fifty followed with questions about why she was wearing them inside and if she'd been assaulted by a boyfriend. Because, of course, only men had the ability to cause black eyes. By the time noon rolled around, she was gratefully accepting the privacy offered to eat in her room, where she caked on even more concealer than usual. Unfortunately, there came a point in her fair complexion where the concealer didn't look so much like concealer as it did a White Chicks façade.

But who cared about beauty points in a situation like this?

She checked her text messages, replied to a concerned Lexi, and a part of her even wished she hadn't insisted her friend return home. Lexi was willing to stick around for a few more days, but as usual, Courtney pushed the caring, sweetly bad-ass girl away. She already had two loves in her broken heart, and she certainly didn't need a third.

By the time evening arrived, Courtney had taken her last dose of Tylenol and was hitching an Uber ride to the nearest mall. She was on the hunt for a new pair of pants. Bloodstains covered her last pair, and even being discreet in the laundry room at the B&B, she couldn't clean them like she should. She was already on a new pair of sneakers since her last tumble in New York; none of her belongings lasted like they did in her old life, and far be it from her to get attached to a silly pair of shoes.

Courtney scoffed at the ridiculous thought. In her old life, long before she'd become this masochistic underground fighter with either a God complex or a death wish — different opinions to different people — she'd freaking loved fashion. She'd loved sexy dresses and cute pumps, six-inch stilettos and glittering rings. The life she was living now just didn't have a whole lot of time, money, or space to keep up her old styles. That didn't mean she didn't long for it from time to time, long for the days when she and Melanie would shop for hours at a time, not necessarily buying up the stores but searching for the perfect outfit or room décor. They'd spend days at the spa, getting massages, facials, and Brazilian waxes. All the things Drew had thought were a bore, her fraternal twin lived for.

That lifestyle didn't suit Courtney any more, it was true, but it certainly didn't stop her from drooling over the silver ballgown on the mannequin she'd almost walked past. It would have fit her elegantly, complimenting her figure without focusing too much on her mere B-cups. She could already see herself wearing it to the next community gala, or Drew's photography award show, or maybe even a wedding…

She mentally smacked herself. She wasn't going there.

Was.

Not.

The fact of the matter was there'd be none of that now. No gala after what she'd been through; no fucking awards show and definitely no fucking wedding. Who was left in her life to go down such a disastrous winding path of misery? Melanie could marry her long-time boyfriend Walker Parkes, but they spent more time being off than on — at least Courtney assumed that was the way it still was. Besides, Melanie had sworn she'd never get married or have kids. And after what happened with Natalie, Courtney was forgoing any notion of marriage ever again. She wasn't planning to get close to another person to hear an *I love you,* let alone ideas of a proposal. Live and learn and all that shit.

Her cell buzzed as she was heading into Sport Chek, and she grinned as she saw Lexi's SMS. *There's another fight coming up. Vance wants u to call him yourself this time, said he was impressed with how much u gave 2 the fight. Take care of urself C, 'cause I'll fly there again if u make me.*

As always, butterflies started taking flight in Courtney's stomach in nervous anticipation of her future fight. The fact that she seemed to lose every other match lately gnawed on her, and she didn't want this fight to be another. For this one she would train harder than ever. She would push herself to the limit. Not because she needed to win for bragging rights, but because she didn't want to lose. She was losing at every other thing in her life; underground fighting didn't have to be one of them.

Chapter 14

Location Undisclosed, April 20

IT TOOK ANOTHER WEEK of training and going through the tedious application process before Courtney was given a time and a place. Each time she wanted to take part in the underground fighting organization, she needed to apply to make sure she was experienced and not about to croak during the match.

Now she stood just outside the ring, glancing around at the low-lit, dank, abandoned building surrounding her. From what she could see, it used to be a commercial property —perhaps a strip mall, but if it hadn't already been shut down due to rodent exposure, it would be condemned now. Thank God Melanie wasn't here; she'd be squealing like a bitch and jumping in any available arms willing to hold her lithe frame. Courtney didn't go to that extreme when she saw mice, or in this case *rats*, but it was certainly making her uneasy. Or maybe it was the musty air she was breathing in; either way, she was having serious regrets about agreeing to fight tonight. What would it matter if she won or lost the match if she was just going to die of lung cancer due to asbestos exposure five years down the road? Did the assholes putting on this event even consider those factors? She doubted it, and the junior operations officer in her wanted to fail these fuckers big-time and send in the Occupational Health and Safety team. And the exterminator.

"Hey, Red."

Courtney froze what she was doing, the zipper to her hoodie halfway down, and for a moment her heart squeezed at the sound of the nickname Kris had given her back when they'd first met. *"If that was a lame-ass attempt at trying to figure out what I am, just ask, Red. I'm a mixture of white, black, and Hispanic races — and I only speak English."*

She spared the guy speaking to her a glance but quickly regretted it. He was a rough one, but what stuck out to her was the disgusting way he grabbed himself and ran his tongue over his lower lip. "Your name's Corey, right? I'm Antoine." He further repulsed her by grinning like a banshee and flashing gold-plated teeth.

Between the creep and the rat she saw earlier, this fucking place was giving her the heebie-jeebies. She turned back to what she was doing, unzipped her hoodie, and pulled the clothing off to stuff into her duffel bag she'd placed at her feet. When she straightened up again, he was still undressing her with his eyes. He must have thought because he ran with a tough crowd he had a right to all women. Well, he had another thing coming.

"What the fuck do you want, Antoine?" she sneered, not in the mood for this shit right before her fight.

He just kept grinning, as if there wasn't currently a fight happening and the crowd pressing in on them wasn't shouting and cheering on the guy winning. "I like your ink. Sexy girl. I bet you like it rough, with whips and chains and shit. I could do whips and chains."

She moved faster than she thought was possible. One minute she was about to tell him off, and the next she was flicking open her Swiss army knife in one hand and grabbing hold of his balls with the other. Her knife hand quivered at his jugular, and the hand cupping his jewels gave a hard squeeze. She never thought she'd be threatening anyone with her knife, and fuck, it terrified her that the desire to kill him was so strong.

"I do it all kinds of ways, but I never fucked a dead guy before. You wanna be my first? I bet it'd be kind of tricky to get your limp dick to stay up if there's no blood there to flow."

To anyone watching, it looked like Courtney had her partially closed fist resting against Antoine's cheek. The blade wasn't easily distinguishable, and as for her hand cutting off the circulation to his nether regions, fuck it. She'd seen more than what appeared to be an intense grope happening at these events. People got straight-up kinky when it came to blood sport.

"You're a crazy bitch." Antoine's gravelly voice was comical. He looked like he was having a rough go in their current arrangement.

"If you ever plan to pick up *any* woman who knows her worth, then you better start by not grabbing your sack as you introduce yourself. It tends to piss us off."

Courtney released him slowly, backing away without taking her eyes off his stunned face. She could hear the current fight ending and knew it was time to go. She picked up her bag from the ground and slung it over her shoulder. It wasn't until she was far away from Antoine that she slipped her knife into the front pocket of her bag. God, her heart was still going crazy! She'd been worried when she bought it that she wouldn't be able to use it, not with what happened to Drew.

By the time she waded through the crowd, the spectators were chanting, already stoked for the upcoming brawl and practically levitating off adrenalin and/or drugs. She ignored the noise, instead concentrating on her movements and her breathing and praying her warm-up before was enough. She caught a flicker of movement from the corner of her eye, and she turned to see her opponent talking with Antoine. She frowned, a bad feeling settling in her stomach. Had he been purposely screwing with her mind to take her attention off the fight? What a dick! Afterward, she'd tell him as much.

She shook her arms loose, stretching her neck from side to side, and flexed both hands. She checked the fitting on her wrist wraps. Sipping her water, she studied her opponent, noting her muscled arms and legs and the mean look she drilled into Courtney. She'd take a wild guess, but she had a feeling Antoine was her man. Or this woman wanted him to be hers. Courtney shook her head, pushing her mouth guard in and unable to fathom Antoine winning the affections of anyone.

The referee got in the middle, saying his peace before declaring the match was started. The moment he stepped back, Courtney's opponent flew into a roundhouse kick. Courtney had just enough time to deflect and laid her fist hard into the girl's back.

They separated, both breathing heavily, and that was when Courtney heard the catcalls and hollers.

"Yeah, baby! You're making me hard, Corey!"

"Kick her ass, Blitz!"

"Blitz, *la faire saigner!*"

"Blitz, make her bleed!" Courtney translated, distraction making her fists come down an inch. Her opponent's name was Blitz?? Seriously? What was wrong with the tough bitches in this city that they had to have such aggressive names? Did their mommy not love them?

She got hit in the face so hard, the force swung her halfway around. She wasn't stable on her feet yet, and Blitz was already kicking her in the hip. As Courtney was stumbling, her previous thought had her inwardly chuckling. Her own mother didn't love her, and she didn't have a crazy ring name.

She quickly turned her fall into a diving roll where she landed on her feet a few steps away. Not taking her eyes off Blitz again, Courtney matched her blow for blow until they were both bleeding. Her head was pounding, pain present behind her eyes; she'd be lying if she said she wasn't worried her concussion had never really left. She'd felt decent the last few days, so she'd been sure she was in the clear. Lexi was going to be pissed if she found out Courtney was fighting with a concussion.

They circled each other, Courtney trying to bounce on her feet just as Natalie had taught her all those months ago. Blitz didn't bounce. In fact, she seemed to charge toward Courtney each time, like she was about to beat her dead into the ground. Her clean attack was lacking, and Courtney knew if they were alone in an alley somewhere, Blitz would no doubt have a pair of brass knuckles and a pipe at her disposal.

Courtney got a strong kick into Blitz's ribs, feeling confident she was evenly matched with the kickboxer. Blitz kicked her thighs a couple times, and then a sharp left hook struck Courtney in the chest. Getting her into a good spot was tough, but when she felt she'd found it she grabbed Blitz's shoulders and drove her knee into her opponent's stomach. She shoved her back and was about to finish her off with a side kick when all hell broke loose in the building.

Frantic shouting assailed her eardrums in every direction, distracting her from the competition. An overwhelming terror washed through her, and she quickly found herself squatting low to the ground, one leg stretched out as she scanned the crowd of spectators. It seemed like the entire house of viewers was scrambling to get away from something, or someone. The place was going fucking nuts. Although she'd guessed it was possible, the makeshift ring around her and Blitz falling down under the horde of people had her shocked still.

"What the fuck?"

She didn't get a chance to stand before they were trampling her, desperate to flee out the back exit. "Hey, watch it!" Courtney cried out as her head hit the hard concrete. A suffocating presence choked her; her mind was fucking with her, and all she could see was Drew. She'd been trying so hard to get to her best friend, but the crowd had been too much at the marathon. She screamed when she felt a sickening snap in her leg, but she was drowned out by the crazies literally stepping on her to escape.

Strong, masculine arms swooped her up just as she was shoving at a woman knocking her around as she ran past. Next thing she knew, she was being tossed over buddy's shoulder, turbulently bouncing off his wide frame as he headed in a different direction, away from anyone else.

Unless someone caught up to them, this bulky threat of a man was going to have Courtney all to himself in no time.

"Hey, hey! Put me down right the fuck now, asshole, or I'm gonna hurl all over you!" Courtney paused in her pounding on his back to grip his sides instead, desperate to hold any part of her steady. Her stomach was terrible, and a cold sweat was soaking her face and neck. She knew she'd broken her leg, and yet all she could focus on was how crampy and disoriented she was. It was as if she was going into stomach flu mode, and her body was prepping her for hours of puking and diarrhea.

"Do what you need to, but I don't plan on putting you down," the man's deep voice called to her over his shoulder. "I don't recommend screaming either, 'cause police are swarming this place, and you'd be on their long list of arrests."

Being arrested is better than dead, though, she thought as he slowed down long enough to shimmy a broken door open. Then they were outside in the fresh air, his footsteps thumping as he bolted down the alleyway. Watching the pavement race by at this angle was making her motion-sick on top of the rest, so she closed her eyes. "Please, put me down. I'll walk wherever but I can't … take much more."

"Courtney, your leg is fucked. Have you seen it? Looks like a snapped chicken bone dangling in your pant leg, now give it a rest."

Courtney? Not Corey? He'd called her Courtney, which meant he'd either dug into her past or he knew her personally. A tingling numbness began from the tips of her fingers down to her toes. Her lips were chattering now, and she knew she was going into shock. Maybe she'd been there all along.

"Looks like I missed the introduction party," she mumbled. She felt rather than saw him lay her down in the back seat of a car. Well, hey, it could've been a trunk. Things were looking up in the world. "You know my name. Who the fuck are you?"

"You don't remember me? Damn, and I thought we'd bonded over flirty conversation and Starbucks."

At the humour in his voice, Courtney dragged her bleary eyes open. The man hovering above her was hazy, but she could make out his unruly brown hair and beefy arms. A handgun was strapped to a shoulder holster. She squinted, finally making out the rest of his gorgeous features.

"Jack?"

Chapter 15

BY THE TIME THEY'D reached the ER, Courtney was blacking in and out. At one point she had a faint knowledge of Jack cradling her in his strong arms and lying his way through the nurse's questions. As she faded out again, she thought she'd heard him say the words *concussion* and *broken ribs*, not leg. That was wrong, she tried to tell him, but she was so exhausted, she couldn't hold her eyes open. She had a broken leg, not broken ribs...

Courtney woke in sheer agony, a sharp cry coming out of her as her gaze flew to the doctor cutting off the pants and shoe on her left leg. "Be gentle, for fuck sakes!"

"Easy, Courtney. There's a lot of swelling," Jack said from beside her. His big hand was gently holding her down in the stretcher.

"It hurts. It fucking hurts, Jack. Why don't you try breaking your fucking leg?" she growled, glaring daggers at him. She was breathing hard, the needle-like sensation in her ribs making it hard to inhale. She made a point of prying his hand off her body and shoving it back to him.

"I did, skiing in the Netherlands. Broke my tibia and fibula in several pieces. They called it a spiral fracture. I've got rods in my leg now," Jack replied patiently. He was speaking to her like a child; God, was she so pathetic right now?

"Boo fucking hoo," she muttered breathlessly. She squinted, the bright lights making her feel like she was watching an alien aircraft land. The illumination kept getting bigger until she couldn't see anything else. Dizziness washed over her, and she shut her eyes to get relief.

"But hey, that was just my leg. You've got a lot more wrong with you," Jack continued with a derisive snort. "So, if you're looking to compare, you win."

The doctor finally got her shoe off, and the pain from her ankle and the swelling made her nauseous. "I'll have the technician take you to X-ray right away," she heard him say in a heavy Quebecois accent.

A tear leaked past her closed eyelids, wetting her eyelashes and cheek in its descent. Getting sensitive like she was would only make it harder to breathe. She pulled her thoughts away from the present drama, instead thinking back on the fight with Blitz and wondering what the hell had happened. Had the cops infiltrated the building, or had a fight broken out? The facts were fuzzy, and all she could really remember was the panicked feeling she'd had with so many people running toward her. She'd been having a serious *Walking Dead* moment, like she was lost in the woods with a horde on her trail. And then in came Jack, her supposed knight in shining armour, but was he really? Honestly, though, why the hell had he even been there? Could it have been just a fluke he was in Montreal at the same time? He worked for her father's security team in California, so unless Sebastian Cairns had hired him to keep tabs...

Another idea formed, one that sent chills down her spine. All those strange instances of someone tailing her sank into her muddled thoughts. She could never get close enough to the man to identify him, but from the one and only time she'd caught sight of the back of him, he'd seemed vaguely familiar. Wide shoulders, wind-blown brown hair and a strong, athletic build she'd once fantasied about having a sexual workout on. Recognition dawned on her seconds before newfound fury erupted inside her.

"Jack."

"Yeah, Courtney?"

She slowly turned her head to cast him a gimlet eye. "What do you think you're doing following me, freak?"

"I'M YOUR BODYGUARD," JACK explained a long while later. They were sitting inside a private room in the ER, waiting for Courtney to go into surgery. Well, he was sitting; she was lying in a bed in a hospital gown.

He said the statement factually, without any sentiment, but Courtney was so high from painkillers, she started to laugh. "That's ... such bullshit. What, are we in a movie?"

Speaking was a workout in itself tonight. She felt asthmatic or like she'd been running on the treadmill for two days straight. On the upside, she could hardly feel her aches and pains due to the strong meds. It made her aware of how tolerant to pain she'd become over the past year, because her limbs hadn't felt this drifty in a long-ass time.

"It's the truth," Jack replied, folding his arms across his chest. "Your father hired me to locate and protect you. He knew of my background in personal security detail and the navy. I'm to protect you from others, but also protect you from yourself. After watching you this last year, I understand why Sebastian included the last bit. I shouldn't have let the fighting go on as long as I did."

"You broke into my apartment. Drugged me," Courtney croaked, suddenly thirsty as fuck. What was she taking again? Morphine? Dilaudids? Oxycodone? Tramadol? A part of her wanted the discomfort back; it didn't cloud her head like the pills did. It was truly no wonder her mother had gotten addicted to this shit. Aleisha Cairns was partial to the tramadol before she got out of bed, and another dose midmorning. By noon she'd be mixing it with oxys, and by supper she was replacing the tramadols with Rita's homemade wine.

Jack had the audacity to nod shamelessly. How she'd ever wanted to bed him, she didn't know. It was like she was meeting him for the first time, and she couldn't stand looking at his military hard edges, let alone hear him speak another condescending word to her. "I did, but it was only to keep you unconscious so I could pop your shoulder back into place and stitch your lip. You didn't seem to have any desire to go to the hospital. I knew you were in a bad way, so I'd gone to check on you, ready to blow my cover. You'd left the curtains in your apartment open, and I found you passed out on your floor, so I let myself in. I could've called your father that night and had you on your way back to Vancouver, but I didn't. I never told him what you were really up to all these months. He thinks you've been backpacking and working with the homeless."

"Fuck you, Jack," Courtney spat. She felt the rage mottling her throat and cheeks, but it was ill-placed because she didn't have the strength to flip him the bird, let alone verbally bulldoze him. She closed her eyes. "Your job is done, the secret is ... out. So, go ... fuck off out of my life."

"I can't just yet," he returned, and a moment later he was close to her, and a drinking straw was pushing against her lips. "Here, take a few sips."

"I thought you liked me, that you were decent." She took the sip before slumping against the pillow. She cracked one eye open in time for his smile.

"I do, and I am, Courtney. I get that you've been having a hard year. I've lost friends too. That's why I didn't feel your father needed to know exactly what was going on. I figured so long as I stayed close, I'd make sure you didn't find yourself in a position you couldn't get out of. It was working, until tonight. I didn't anticipate a sting and stampede."

"You and me both," she mumbled, drowsy. She didn't think it'd be possible to sleep again with her migraine, but as soon as Jack was silent for a few minutes, she was drifting off.

Chapter 16

"I'VE GOT THREE FRACTURED ribs, a sprained ankle, a clean break in my left tibial bone, and a moderate concussion," Courtney told Lexi over FaceTime the next day. She watched her friend sketch a design on her iPad as she listened.

Lexi shook her head, glancing up to give Courtney a sympathetic look. "That sucks! I guess you should be happy you made it out of there at all. I heard a bunch of people got arrested. Two people were shot, but it was gang-related, nothing to do with the cops."

"That's crazy. You know what else? I was having … a bad feeling yesterday, like I shouldn't … be fighting."

"Some premonition shit right there," Lexi replied. She began sketching the dog's nose. "So what will you do, go home? Might not be a bad idea. Stop running, you know. You've got a company to take over one day. Can't do that if you're dead."

Courtney grimaced, hitting the recline button on her hospital bed. The cast on her leg was driving her batty; it was itchy and made her uncomfortable all over. Her ribs made movement a strenuous task, and every time she spoke or breathed it hurt her chest. "I regret telling you that," she muttered, but she didn't really. She'd missed connecting with people on a personal level, and she figured if she was genuinely going to be Lexi's friend, then she should divulge a few things.

"Don't dodge my question, beautiful girl. You're welcome to recuperate at my place, and I swear I'll do my best to behave. Or you can grow a set of ironclad lady balls and face your past. The anniversary is coming up soon."

Courtney blinked, knowing Lexi was right but hating that she was. She'd been running for so long, trying to forget who she'd been and become someone else. The problem was, life didn't work like that. Her baggage followed, and in the process of being haunted either by beautiful or bittersweet memories, she was somehow losing the good in her too. She'd never guessed she'd become so indifferent, uncaring for herself or those around her. She'd been hot-headed before, but she'd also been the kind of person people could depend on. Drew's last words had been a testament to that fact, asking Courtney to love Kris and their daughter Cadence as she'd loved Drew. Her best friend had known she was dying, and her last wish before she left earth was for Courtney to help her family.

God, Drew would be rolling over in her grave if she knew what Courtney had become.

"Hey, where'd you go? You look like you're somewhere else," Lexi said, pulling Courtney back to the present. She'd finished her sketch and had carried her cell over to her tattoo station. She was currently sanitizing all the equipment.

Courtney shook her head and winced. Out of all her injuries, the concussion currently had to be the worst. "Just thinking about her. You're right; I know you are."

"Finally! You're listening to the voice of reason." Lexi laughed. She had her bare leg exposed on the table, but when she turned on the tattoo gun, the noise grated through Courtney's head so bad, her eyes crossed. "What's the deal with that Jack creep? He still around?"

Courtney's stomach did a vicious roll, and she gave a hard swallow. "He's not so bad, but yeah. He somehow ... saved my bag from the building while carrying me out. And went to my Workaway this morning ... whew." She paused, sweat dotting her forehead. There was just too much going on with her body right now. It was an overload of raw sensation. She rested her hand on her chest, trying to breathe. "Jack talked them into giving him all my stuff. Said I wouldn't be back."

"Fuck, that guy is way too convincing. I don't know how someone could lie so well and so often. He must be pathological."

Courtney was going to be sick. "Lex, awesome tat you're making, but I gotta let you go."

Lexi glanced up at her, confused. "Oh, okay. Bye. Keep me posted."

"Uh-huh." Courtney hurriedly pressed the *end call* button. She barely had time to grab the spit dish, and she was throwing up. This was worse than any hangover she'd ever had, worse than the Hellevator at Playland.

There was a knock on the door before it opened and a nurse came in. She saw Courtney heaving — now missing the tiny bowl altogether — and hit the call button for help. "*Bonjour*, Courtney, *je m'appelle* Jacinta. I will help you?"

Courtney instinctually nodded and then puked some more. The entire room was spinning, and if she could, she'd go back in time and kick her own ass for being in the wrong place at the wrong time.

The woman washed her hands before prying the useless dish from Courtney's grip. In exchange, a proper bowl was set in front of her. She focused on the circular object the best she could to hopefully fade out the background tilt-a-whirl happening in her peripheral vision. Another nurse came in, and they gently pulled her sheets off and then removed her hospital gown. She was pissed she wasn't more helpful, embarrassed she'd just puked all over herself, and she wasn't even drunk.

"Don't worry. The vertigo should pass in a few days as your concussion gets better," the second nurse said to her in clearer English than the first. On a good brain day, she most likely would encourage them to speak French to her. She loved languages, had learned French, Spanish, Portuguese, and German before she'd graduated high school. Today, though, she was doing well not to piss the bed while she puked. Maybe tomorrow she'd be feeling well enough to impress them with her skills.

Jack returned when the nurses were finishing washing her up. He at least had the manners to bashfully turn away when he saw they hadn't put her johnny shirt on yet. Him seeing her half naked was the least of her worries. She was more humiliated of her sick stomach than flashing him with her perky boobs.

"Sorry, Courtney, I should've knocked louder." He faced the wall. "Just wondering what the plan is? I overheard the doctor saying he'd let you leave in another day or two. Should I make arrangements, or will I be following you around a different part of the world this time?"

The johnny shirt on, and Courtney rested her head back on the pillow. She couldn't globe-trot in this condition. What was the point anymore? She'd started out angry at the world, desperate to do damage. But now? She was so, so tired, and if she was being honest, she missed her father and her friends like crazy. She missed Rita, mama Jen, and Cadence, even Liz and Peter. Drew's family had become hers as well over the years.

With Drew's pleading request foremost in her mind, she said, "Take me home, Jack. But we're driving and getting two separate hotel rooms. And you're paying."

"Of course, Miss. Cairns," Jack replied, turning to face her as the nurses left the room. He gave a slight bow, but he was grinning. "Glad to have you on board again."

Chapter 17

Shaughnessy Heights, Vancouver, May 5

DESPITE ALL HER PREVIOUS self-talk, she didn't tell anyone she was home for the first week. Apart from her father and house staff at his mansion, no one knew Courtney was in Vancouver. She hadn't felt up to company, still humiliated she was beat to hell, and honestly, lying to her father was hard enough. Lexi had been right about her lacking a poker face. Courtney would have told him the truth had Jack not already created a half-truth of her being trampled — but at a concert.

When Sebastian received word she was in the city and coming home — not the condo she'd shared with Natalie — he'd surprised Courtney by cancelling his meetings for the remainder of the day. It was he who had opened the gate and greeted her and Jack at the front door. She probably would have gone back to the condo to heal by herself, except amid her heartache over Drew, she'd signed the property over to Natalie. She'd since found out all her stuff had been shipped back to the mansion, so go figure.

It felt strange to be in her old room again. The space was enormous, larger even then her tiny apartment in NYC. She had changed in her year away. She felt too small in her bedroom; a stranger, viewing possessions that no longer held the same significance they once did. Rita, their family housekeeper, had taken it upon herself to open the storage boxes from the condo and put her things away. She'd always been sweet like that, caring for Courtney whether she wanted or needed it.

She was soaking in a bubble bath Sunday afternoon, broken leg propped over the side, when there was a knock on the bathroom door. Rita popped her head in, "*Lista para salir, querida?*"

Courtney smiled, appreciating the fact Rita always felt comfortable speaking Spanish with her. Originally from Ecuador, she'd been with the family since Courtney was a child. She was more like family than staff in Courtney's eyes, and Rita was the reason she'd become so absorbed in different cultures and their language. Rita herself had taught Courtney how to speak her mother tongue. "*Si, lista. Ya estoy tan arrugada como una pasa.*" *Yes, ready. I'm as wrinkled as a prune now.*

"Are you still going to see Drew's mami?" Rita asked in English now. She reached into the bath water to pull the drain stopper up.

Courtney gave her a solemn nod. She'd been high and low all morning with her feelings, getting upset and then scolding herself for it. She prided herself on being strong of mind and heart, but since she'd landed home, she found her armour cracking. Tomorrow would be the one-year anniversary, and she wanted to visit with mama Jen to see if anything had been arranged. Either way, it was important to her she be there for Jen. As difficult as it no doubt would be on all of them.

With Rita supporting most of her weight, Courtney managed to lift up and onto the tub ledge. She was grateful she no longer suffered from vertigo, but she still had another couple of weeks to fully heal from the concussion. When she got turned around with her legs on the floor of the bathroom, Rita passed her the crutches.

"Thank you." She gratefully accepted the help, tucking them under her armpits before carefully standing. Her torso groaned in complaint, but she'd learned since her stint in the hospital to breathe slowly through it.

"So many bruises, *querida*," Rita whispered, wrapping a large terrycloth towel around Courtney's shoulders. Unlike with her father, Courtney had told Rita the truth about her whereabouts the past year. And why wouldn't she? Rita had been more of a mother to Courtney than her own mother over the years. She'd lost count how many occasions she'd been nursed back to health from a cold or flu or even a hangover. Rita never judged her meanly, like Aleisha Cairns would all too often do. If she ever used a judging tone with Courtney, it was more out of disappointment than ridicule or resentment.

"I'm sure I would have won that match," Courtney muttered, hobbling over to her daybed, where Rita had graciously chosen an outfit for her. She'd always been over-the-top, going well beyond her job duties, probably from missing her family in Ecuador. She visited them once a year, sometimes two if Courtney's father was feeling generous with his Christmas bonuses, but she always said the time spent there was never enough.

"What I don't understand is why didn't you run with them? You saw them coming at you, no? Why wait until they trample you?"

"I–I froze, panicked," Courtney admitted, silently accepting Rita's help pulling on a pair of low-rise panties. She closed her eyes briefly, thinking back on the insanity in that abandoned building. "I felt like it was happening all over again."

"You must have been so scared. My poor *querdio*."

"Yeah."

When she was all dressed, Rita left her to go switch the laundry over. Courtney hobbled over to her makeup table, pulling out the chair and slowly lowering herself on it. She picked up her brush, taking her time combing out the tangles in her curls. And even after she'd applied her makeup, she still felt horribly out of place in her childhood home. Was it that she no longer belonged there, or would it just take some getting used to again?

She had no idea, no fucking clue where she belonged.

Chapter 18

B.C. Psychiatric Care Facility, May 9

"YOU CAN GO RIGHT in, Ms. Cairns," the nurse said with an encouraging smile. Her hand was on the door, waiting for Courtney to cross the threshold. "Although he *has* come out of it a few times, you'll most likely be seeing him in his catatonic state."

Courtney nodded, taking a deep breath. "Dr. Matheson mentioned he's ... inconsolable when he awakens. Is this true?"

"I haven't seen it myself, but it appears so." She grimaced. "If you need anything, or if he does wake up, there are a few orderlies in the rec room as well."

I've got this. Totally. No problem, Courtney silently rehearsed. She stepped cautiously inside, pleasantly taken aback at how much natural light shone in through the large window. She scanned over the many faces until she found him in the far corner. He sat in a wheelchair, facing the window, as if he were looking out at the flower gardens below. As she neared him, however, she quickly found it wasn't the case. There was an absence in his brown gaze — an almost lifeless feeling about him. The facial scar he'd received from the attack cut through his beard like a streak through wet paint. It made him look unhinged, or could be it only added to the dangerous aura he'd had all along. The scar began a few inches from his chin on his right side, just below his jaw, effectively splitting into his bottom lip. Courtney's eyes stung as she vividly remembered that fateful day, and for a moment she wondered if perhaps she shouldn't have come here. She'd known it would be difficult to face Kris, but she hadn't anticipated seeing Drew when she looked at him.

Swallowing the lump in her throat, she tried to shake off her sudden unease and pulled up a chair in front of him. She lowered herself down with the crutches before tucking them off to the side, out of the way. She zeroed in on Kris's head, on the rough haircut just above his ears. She supposed the staff must have been cutting his hair; from the little mama Jen had told her, it didn't sound as if she came in to see him too often.

She reached for his hands folded in his lap. "Hey, bad ass," she murmured, watching his eyes in hope of some flicker of recognition. He never moved; really, the only indication he was even alive was his relaxed exhales that fanned her cheek.

"I should have come sooner — I'm sorry about that," she told him, casting her eyes to the floor. "I've had a hell of a year. After what happened with ... you know, I ran; like I always fucking do. I'll try to find pictures to show you sometime, because I doubt you'd believe what I've been up to since you saw me last." She gestured to her cast. "I don't know if you can see me in there, but I'm pretty broken up from being in the wrong place at the wrong time. Like you in that convenience store, remember? Except while you were pulling the hero act, I was ... yeah. Underground fighting is definitely not a hero-of-the-day-lesson." Courtney grimaced before taking a sip of her water. "It's not much to brag about, but I'd put money on it you'd laugh your ass off at the stories. You're twisted that way."

She heaved a sigh. "Truth is, I was lost for a while too. I disappeared, trying to find where I fit in the world without baby girl. For so many years I woke up and couldn't wait to see her, you know? Well, yeah, you know what I'm talking about. And now it's gone, everything is. She's just snatched ... right the fuck out of our lives. It's not fair. I think I'd actually kill to see her smile or hear her laugh again. Just one more time, but in real time. Not watching it from a goddamn video."

Voicing aloud everything she felt to Kris was somehow comforting. He couldn't get pissed or judgmental about her feelings or misgivings; as far as she could tell, he wasn't even hearing her. She gathered her thoughts and studied him once more. He seemed frail inside his loose-fitting white t-shirt and black sweatpants. The slippers were a stark contrast to the workboots he always used to wear. The entire outfit made him seem off-colour — not at all like the athletic basketball devotee who would spend his free time doing chin-ups to calm his racing thoughts.

She cleared her throat, absently rubbing her thumb across the back of his hand. Before life as they'd both known it crumbled before their eyes, Kris would have taken this opportunity to say something arrogantly flippant. He'd have glanced down at her, batted those gallingly long eyelashes, and demanded to know why she was giving him such a show of feeling. Courtney divulging her vulnerable state just wasn't done, and he'd certainly have called her on it.

But that was before. Today was different. Today she at least needed to pretend he was listening. She gazed into his espresso eyes, wishing he would look at her. She considered all the months she'd spent hating him, blaming him for Drew's death. Like everyone did, she'd gone through the usual stages of grief. When she'd reached the anger stage, she thought long and hard of different ways she might kill the man sitting before her now. Poison his chocolate milk, tie him up and slit his wrists, beat him to death with her bare hands ... for a while she'd let her newfound hatred consume her. It'd eaten away at her like a piranha to her insides, and then she'd kicked a drunk guy over his chair in a New York bar. It was there she'd found her fighting outlet from connections through Maxine. It'd saved her more than she could ever put into words. Looking at Kris now, the hatred was long gone. Whether or not Drew was dead because of his actions didn't change the way Courtney felt about him, about their shared tragedy. She knew Kris had perhaps loved Drew more than even she had. Hating him for something neither of them could change was both tiring and futile. She'd rather remain his friend and make sure he didn't kill himself when he woke up.

Kris still sat in the same position, unmoving, slow breaths flowing in and out of his nose. She studied his hands, realizing she'd never held them before, or couldn't remember if she had. They were darker than hers, the difference between apricot and golden-tanned, and despite the scars they held, they were beautiful. Large basketball hands with long, graceful fingers.

"Monday marked one year since we lost baby girl," she murmured, gently turning over the hand with the bullet scar and massaging the palm. A tear dropped onto her arm, but she didn't reach to brush it away. Let them fall. She'd held on as long as she could today. "I went with mama Jen and Cadence out to the ranch to see Liz and Peter. For a tribute, we decided to uh … do a photo shoot in Drew's honour. We used her camera, and I'm planning to develop them this week. I watched baby girl mix the solutions for years so," more tears fell, "I figure if we did this every anniversary, I could develop them. I think it's what she would want."

Kris's hand twitched, startling her. She glanced up, alarmed to find him slowly blinking as he became aware. "Red?" he mumbled faintly. He stared across at her with those beguiling brown eyes, completely dazed.

"Kris. You're awake," she exclaimed, a gush of relief racing past her lips. She grabbed hold of her crutches, getting to her feet as quickly as she could before she threw her arms around him. "I can't believe it!"

"Don't squeeze so … hard, muscles," Kris replied, a slight slur in his deep baritone. He frowned at her cast. "What the fuck happened to you?"

Courtney swallowed, so stunned to hear his voice that she found herself stammering, "I–I got trampled. It's a long story — did you not hear anything I've been saying?"

Kris glanced around them, a peculiar look on his bearded face. "Bits and pieces, like a dream. Where the hell are we, Red? My–my memory's fucked, like it's been through a blender. I don't remember a lot. Your hair seems longer."

"Can't slip anything past you, can I?" she replied thickly. She slid her chair closer to him, and as she took a seat once more, she noticed a few of the staff watching them with a distinct interest. They'd no doubt be interrupting their reunion in no time.

"Why am I here, Red? Fuck, I'm so weak; can barely lift my arm," Kris muttered, half to himself.

"It's so good to hear your voice," Courtney said, selfishly wishing they were somewhere private so she could have him to herself for a few minutes. Besides Melanie, he was the only friend she'd seen so far from ... before; she'd felt so alone in her mourning.

He sluggishly grasped her arm, opening his mouth to say something, and then froze. He very carefully raised his free hand to his face, his fingers slipping over the scar tissue. A surprised gasp escaped him.

"There was an accident," Courtney began, almost soundlessly. She found herself reaching for his jaw as well, her hand covering his in some semblance of comfort.

A frightened look crossed his face, and his gaze flew up to meet hers. "Where's my girls? Dobie did this, I just know it. Fuck, I–I shouldn'tve told Ace where they could find him. Where's D at? Gotta make sure he don't try nuttin'."

Tears blurred Courtney's vision as she held him still. She clutched his shoulder for support. "She's gone, Kris."

"Gone? What ya mean, gone?"

"Drew isn't—" Her voice broke, so she gave her head a slight shake. "There's only Cadence left."

"Only Cadence ... Red, that can't be," Kris insisted, panic setting a hard edge to his tone. He tried to stand up, but the weakness in his legs kept him rooted to the wheelchair. His shoulders began to tremble under her hand, and then she saw tears streaming down his face. "She swore she'd never leave me."

"Dobie tried to ... but baby girl saved you. Saved Cadence," Courtney choked out, unable to say the words.

"No. No ... no, please Red, no," Kris pleaded, his hands on her arms as he stared at her. He was blubbering, broken all over again as the truth sank in.

She wrapped her arms around him the best she could once more, and he sobbed into her chest, his hands clinging to her hips for dear life. Courtney closed her eyes, just as a fresh tear escaped. She brushed it away and then smoothed her hand down his back as he cried. She didn't say anything; she didn't have to. Words were beyond them, both lost in thoughts of Drew. After a few minutes, Kris's sobs quieted, and then a moment later they silenced altogether. She pulled away to find him empty gazing to the window behind her, once again in his catatonic state. The rims of his eyes were red and bloodshot from crying, and a lone tear dribbled from the corner of his eye.

She swallowed the lump lodged in her throat, pushing him back more in his wheelchair. *Fuck, so you just cop out and get to disappear again?* she thought, twisting away from him to smack her hand against the table beside them. She successfully got the attention of half the room, and now her palm stung; she only wished she could have punched Kris instead. Her breaths were laboured as she bit out, "You're leaving me here to mourn her alone again. Fuck, Kris — I need you right now. I need my friend back."

Her hand trembled as she hastily snatched up her backpack, ready to get the hell out of there. Kris sat so still, but the continual tears escaping him made her question if he was truly catatonic. "I lost her too, don't forget. I loved her so much, for so long, and I didn't think I'd last one week without hearing her say my name."

She reached for her crutches, shaking her head in disbelief as she stood up. She was so pissed, and, if she were honest, jealous that he got to just block out all the hurt she'd had to go through over Drew's death. "The last thing Drew asked of me was to love you and Cadence the way I loved her," she whispered. She looked down at him with a tearful admission. "But I don't think I could. Drew was special and ... honestly, I don't think I want to open myself to that again. Seeing you locked inside your own pain is helping me realize how stupid I was for coming home. I think you had it right, bad ass. It's safer not to feel at all. And if we can't be there for each other, then I'm out. It hurts too fucking much to be around you."

She gave him one last, lingering look before hobbling away on her crutches. She'd made it out of the rec room and into a private restroom before she cracked. She collapsed on the toilet seat, pain racing up her side and down her leg, but it was her heart splintering. Her hand pressed against her chest, the other clasped over her mouth to keep her sobs at bay.

Fuck, she hadn't anticipated seeing Kris again would be this gut-wrenching. The wounds she'd placed band-aids over had fallen off, leaving behind a steady stream of fresh despair and longing in its wake. She'd been stupid to think a band-aid would fix such a deep cut; all fighting had done was suppress her heartache enough to function and rid her of some of her anger.

A knock sounded on the door. "Everything all right in there? You've been in there a while."

"Yup fine. I'm coming right out," she shakily replied. She grabbed some toilet paper off the roll and blew her nose. Then she washed her hands in the sink and splashed cold water on her cheeks and eyes. Dabbing the wetness away with paper towel, she reluctantly left the confines of the restroom. When the woman waiting in the hall saw her, she moved aside to let Courtney go by with the crutches. With her skin tone, it was obvious to anyone within eyesight range that she'd been crying, but she just kept her face averted to the floor as much as possible on the way out of the facility. As soon as she was in the back seat of her father's company car, she pulled her cell from her backpack. "Take me home please, Roger."

"Certainly, Ms. Cairns."

She pulled up Lexi's number and sent her a text she'd no doubt regret later. A long time later. *I could really use a friend atm. Any chance u have a desire to come to Van? I can email u a plane ticket.* Of all the thousands of people in her city she could and should seek comfort from, she was selfishly asking Lexi. Fuck, she was just like Kris. Worse even, because she was intelligent enough to know better.

She was nearing home when she got a reply. *Sure, u okay? I can buy my own ticket if I can crash with u.*

Sounds good. Thanx Lex. She didn't think her father would approve of Lexi, but luckily the mansion was enormous, so she shouldn't have any trouble sneaking her in. She felt a little guilty, though, like she was using Lexi, but she had an inkling her friend didn't mind it at all. *Can u bring ur tattoo stuff?*

Yups. Be there by midnight. Gotta cancel some clients. See u soon.

Chapter 19

"I'M NOT FUCKING YOU tonight," Lexi murmured in her ear many hours later.

Courtney scowled, turning into her on the bed. "Why the hell not?" She was all too aware she sounded like the spoiled rich girl she was, but fuck, if they weren't going to have sex, what did Lexi fly all this way for?

Her friend chuckled, her breath tickling Courtney's ear as she lay next to her. Lexi caressed her cheek, tracing her tattooed fingers over her the shape of her mouth. "Because," she returned, laughter still present in her voice as she bent to replace her fingers with her lips. Her tongue ring licked at her entrance, but Courtney clamped her lips closed tight. She was sexually frustrated and emotionally spent — so not in the mood for mind games.

"Tonight, I need to save you from yourself," Lexi said, moving her hand to Courtney's hair, not at all offended that Courtney rejected her kiss. She twirled the long tendrils around her finger. "I'll gladly give you fresh ink; a tattoo will do the same as sex when it comes to absolving any emotional shit going on. I won't have sex with you, though; you're too fucking rowdy, and baby, I don't know if you've noticed, but you could end up back in the hospital if I fuck you. One good spasm could fracture your ribs more."

"Then why are you here, Lexi?" Courtney bit out, not caring one iota if she hurt her feelings. She pushed her hand off her shoulder and yanked back the sheets to get out of bed.

"Hey, hey, where you going, beautiful girl?" Lexi asked, sitting up as well. Her hand shot to Courtney's arm, holding her still. "Are you telling me you'd rather I not care about hurting you more? Do you think I'd province-hop just to get laid? I can do that at home. If you wanted callous, you should've gone to the bar and picked up there. But you didn't. You asked for me."

"Big mistake, I see now," Courtney retorted, so distraught at this point, she was practically levitating off the bed. She couldn't pummel someone in the ring due to her injuries, and now Lexi wasn't giving it up in bed because of them. What the fuck gave, honestly?

"C'mere, please. I don't think I'm explaining this right." Lexi tugged on her hand, and Courtney slowly turned into her, careful not to twist too fast. Lexi splayed her hand over her hip, catching the hem of her tank between her fingers. Their eyes met. "You're my friend, and although I have plenty of them, you're one of my closest these days. I feel like I get you, that we understand each other. I don't fuck all my friends, and generally I don't become friends with the girls I'm with. But being a part of your life is a no-brainer, Courtney. It's one of those things I'm all too happy to be a part of. I came all the way here because I care, and it's not rocket science to see how much you're hurting. Despite what you've learned or been taught, there's healthier ways to deal with heartache than what you've been doing."

Courtney cleared her throat as she processed everything Lexi said. It felt like she was on display, each one of her shortcomings wide open for Lexi to see. She knew what Courtney sought, what she *craved*, what she'd *begged* Lexi to fly to Vancouver for, and yet not only did she boldly refuse her, she wanted to — to what? Counsel her? Hug her while she cried? Well, that shit was *never* happening. There was only one person in the entire world who was ever able to wring a confession from her, and he was currently a breathing corpse locked inside his own fucking drama. Not exactly an incentive to have circle time; if Kris going to therapy all that time had still made him crack in the end, what hope did she have?

"Lexi," she said in a tone so stiff, she didn't recognize it, "if you're wanting me to talk about my feelings, then you're wasting your time. I'd rather sew my eyelids to my fucking eyebrows."

"That's intense."

"Yeah, well, I haven't had sex in almost a month, and besides beating on someone, it's my most effective stress reliever," Courtney snapped. She shrugged her touch off again, this time succeeding in sitting up. She reached for her crutches, lifting herself to a standing position and heading to the bathroom.

"What are you doing?"

"What do you think? I'm going to the bar. I plan for some lucky guy to be balls-deep inside me in less than an hour." She slammed the bathroom door so hard, it hurt more than her ears. Her breath caught as sharp prickles raced up her ribcage and stabbed her in the chest. She stared at her reflection in the mirror, momentarily hung up on the rage staining her throat and cheeks a rosy hue. She was shaking, withdrawing from she didn't know what, but she had a suspicion it ended in an orgasm. Fuck, she was going crazy. Was she really going to ditch Lexi, head across the city to find some random guy to get her rocks off?

"God, I miss you, baby girl," she whispered to the ceiling. Her soft voice cracked under the pressure, and it took a while longer before she felt composed enough to head back into her bedroom. Lexi had moved off the bed and over to Courtney's tabletop, where she often worked and ate her meals when she didn't feel like eating alone down in the formal dining room. Sometimes she ate in the kitchen with the staff, but she was often too busy for that.

She watched as Lexi patiently disinfected all her tattooing supplies, carefully setting them down on the prepped table, which was now plastic-wrapped. She was getting ready to tattoo someone, Courtney, if she wanted it. A shiver of excitement coursed through Courtney as she remembered the pain from her rib tat. She inched forward on her crutches, taking note of the book-size flash sheets Lexi had brought with her. Courtney picked it up wordlessly, scanning through the sketches for a few minutes until she found one she liked. And then she found two more.

"I want you to give me half a sleeve; will you do it?"

Lexi stared, her blue eyes perplexed. When she spoke, all she said was, "Tattoos are hard to remove, even with your kind of resources. So make sure you're not gonna regret what you pick and where I put it."

"Do you not think I'll look good with a half sleeve? You look great with yours."

"That's the least of my worries. I think I'll be half in love with you with a sleeve," Lexi huskily admitted. She dropped her gaze away from Courtney's, adding, "It's just you didn't spend too much time looking for a design. I could make one for you, if you like. I'll do it for free, even. So long as you're not running around half-cocked looking to get your other leg broken, or worse, pregnant with a kid you don't want."

"I want the upper half of my arm done. I've actually been thinking about it for a long time. And I'm sorry. I can be cruel sometimes, and I know you're trying to help me," Courtney said, ashamed of the way she'd acted.

"It's okay. I'm made of tougher stuff than what you can dish out," Lexi replied, wrapping her arm around Courtney's waist. She gave a gentle tug, and Courtney took a seat on her lap. It was an awkward feat with her cast, but as soon as she was comfortable, Lexi gave her a sweet kiss. It wasn't a joining with promises of sex, or a breakup, and it wasn't a kiss that got Courtney revving for the high she craved. It was an honest-to-goodness affectionate kiss from someone whose heart she would likely shatter.

"One day," Lexi whispered between kisses, "I wanna hook up with you when you've had an awesome day, and everything went right."

Courtney bit her lip, resting her forehead on Lexi's shoulder. She reluctantly murmured, "He woke up today. The fucker snapped out of his catatonic state, long enough to cry over Drew and disappear again. I–I can't do it, Lexi. I don't know why I came back here. It's too hard to face the past."

One of Lexi's hands began slow circles on Courtney's back. She was fighting back tears again, angry that she was so distraught today. It wasn't like her; it usually took quite a lot for her to cry.

"Running again isn't the answer," Lexi said quietly. She tilted Courtney's tearful gaze up to meet the kindness in hers. "Ever think that facing Kris, facing what happened, is the way for both of you to heal? You know, maybe you need him as much as he needs you. You guys were good friends, were you not? He's caged in his mind just like you, unable to move on. Running away to your next fight won't change that."

Courtney felt her bottom lip tremble, and she swallowed the lump lodged in her throat. She glanced away, not wanting Lexi to see her cry. "Then what? I'm supposed to keep going back there? You think I–I should keeping torturing myself by seeing him? For how fucking long?"

"For as long as it takes, beautiful girl. Just for as long as it takes."

Chapter 20

AN INDULGENT SIGH ESCAPED Courtney as her traitorous body relaxed against Lexi's insistent hold on her waist, her back nestling into her chest. Lexi's soft lips rained gentle kisses along Courtney's throat and shoulder. What could she say? It'd been a long-ass morning at work, hobbling around on one leg. She'd been making her appearances inside Cairns Corp. short and sweet since she'd arrived home. Not just to ease herself back into the fold, but also to ease the board into the idea of giving her a second chance. Or was it her third?

Her eyes fluttered closed against her will, and the passing scenery faded outside the company car. The conflicting bullshit about it was, she could totally get used to this; she felt all too good in Lexi's arms. "You've never done the friends with benefits thing before, have you?" Her breath fanned Lexi's cheek as she craned her face around.

Lexi grinned, looking hot as fuck in her aviator shades. Hers were so similar to the pair Drew used to wear, but she wore them differently. Whereas Drew had achieved the adorable girl-next-door look, Lexi oozed confidence in her sex appeal. She'd spent the morning riding the Sky Train and getting her hair dyed as she'd waited for Courtney. "Nope," She replied, overpronouncing the "p" so the word popped out between her lips.

Well, that figured. "I hate to be the one to tell you, but you're failing miserably." Lexi's kiss landed on her mouth this time, quickly pushing the pause button on their conversation.

"Like I said the other night, I'm never friends with women I fuck. For the most part, I hang with the guys; you know, other tattooists or with Chad and them. In my experience, women come with too much drama."

"And yet I'm the exception to your case." Lexi's free hand slipped into the waistband of her pencil skirt, and when she rubbed her finger along Courtney's slit a moment later, she couldn't hold back the moan. Her pussy clenched so hard, she grabbed Lexi's arm to still her movements.

"Unless you're planning to follow through, stop teasing," she warned tightly. She still hadn't gotten over the other night; Lexi hadn't come to Vancouver to get laid, and she made certain Courtney knew it every chance she got.

"We've got an audience," Lexi voiced against her ear, retracting her hand only to place both on Courtney's tummy.

Distracted by those hands moving up her torso to cup her breasts, it took a hot second for Lexi's words to sink in. When they did, Courtney's gaze flew to the rear-view mirror to greet Roger's, and the old perv seemed prepared to go off the road rather than look away.

"So we do." Courtney reached up and snaked her hand around Lexi's head, pulling her in for another kiss. Her tone teased as she called out to her driver, "Eyes on the road, Roger."

She'd spent her whole life trying to be someone she wasn't, trying to appease everyone's opinions. The only time she'd ever allowed her steely exterior to crack was when she was drunk. But she wasn't the same girl she'd been a year ago; today she felt bold, daring, and if Lexi was into giving old Roger a little show, then she was so down.

"You dress different here," Lexi murmured, tugging at Courtney's bottom lip with her teeth. The top two buttons on her teal blouse came undone, and Courtney watched from under hooded eyes as Lexi's fingers pushed the fabric open to expose the red lace bra underneath.

"Different good?" she wondered, guiding her mouth back to hers. She held Lexi's face in her hands, securing her in place for her kiss. Her lips boldly moved over Lexi's, pushing them apart and taking what she wanted. Her tongue stroked Lexi's bottom lip, tasting the caramel frappuccino she'd finished on their drive. Nothing had changed since the other night; she was still horny as fuck and completely aware of Lexi's skilled fingers continuing to undo her blouse one button at a time. Then her hand was gently closed over Courtney's throat, her thumb intimately stroking Courtney's increasing pulse and her fingers pressing the back of Courtney's neck, abruptly taking charge of the kiss. Her tongue brushed against Lexi's barbell, and the slight scraping it caused had insane desire shooting straight to the burning heat between her legs.

The hell with having an audience, Courtney thought, scrambling to press the button for the privacy screen. When Roger was safely out of sight, she unbuckled and carefully shifted in her seat. Her ribs were doing better, but she didn't want to push it. Lexi's baby blues watched intensely as Courtney awkwardly sprawled out in the backseat, her good leg propped up and the one in the cast resting on the floor.

"Different good," Lexi huskily replied finally, unbuckling as well. "You're fucking sexy, and I can see your ink through the blouse. Your arm especially." She draped her body precariously over Courtney's and made a beeline for her open blouse. She nuzzled her face into Courtney's breasts — her newly bleached, much shorter hair momentarily drawing Courtney's attention. She didn't think it was possible for Lexi to not look sinfully sexy. Her nipples were two stiffened peaks, begging for the persistence of Lexi's tongue. She was unzippering Lexi's biker jacket when she heard a muttered curse.

"I'm fucking stuck."

"You're what?" Courtney asked in confusion, immediately gripping Lexi's shoulders to push her off.

Lexi's hand flew up, halting her in her tracks. "Wait! My nose ring is caught on your bra, beautiful girl. It'd be a bitch to heal if it got yanked out."

Courtney angled her head to the side, and sure enough, the hoop ring in Lexi's nose was hooked into her lace. She groaned, her head falling back on the seat, and she glared up at the car roof. "I'm just not meant to have sex with this broken leg, am I? Why is the universe being so goddamn cruel to me?"

Despite the predicament they were in, Lexi started laughing. She reached one hand up to feel for Courtney's lips, then caressed her fingers over them. "If you could quit the pity party and help untangle me, I'll give you the sex, beautiful girl. You've already won."

She sounded genuine over her defeat, and that had Courtney calming down a little. She peered down at Lexi, whose eyes were straining to see her in the uncomfortable position she rested in. "Promise?"

Lexi rolled her eyes. "Do we need to do a spit handshake on it? Fuck, beautiful girl, your bra's nice an all, but I'd rather have it on the floor."

Just then Courtney felt the car rumbling to a stop. With Lexi draped over her, she couldn't see out the window. She heard the car door closing, and then a moment later a knock sounded on the back window. Her eyes widened. *Shit!* she mouthed to Lexi, who in turn laughed again, harder this time. Great fucking help she was gonna be.

"Ms. Cairns, we've arrived on location."

"Roger, hi. We'll be a moment, okay?" Courtney called, stifling a giggle as well now.

"Okay. Also, your father has me keeping a travel log. Would you rather I left this one out?"

That had her frowning. "I don't give a shit if he knows where we are." To Lexi she whispered, "Where are we?"

"Shooting range," Lexi replied with a shit-eating grin.

Courtney reeled back in surprise, that answer not being in her top five. "Oh. Of course we are."

"Let's sit up at the same time; that way you can help me get out of your bra."

She snickered but readied herself all the same. "We'll have to go slow because of my cast. One ..."

"Two..."

"Three!"

"It's really not that bad," Courtney told her once they were both upright. She gently reached for Lexi's nose ring.

"Not great either, though. At least you smell good," Lexi rumbled.

"Hold still." Courtney bit her lip in concentration and carefully worked the ring out of the lacy cleavage part on her bra. When Lexi's unique features came into clear view once more, she was wrapping her in a hug before she could stop herself. Lexi felt good in her arms, and Courtney found herself playing the reminder over and over in her head that they were just friends. Hearts had no say in this.

Courtney cleared her throat, uneasily dropping her arms away. She opened the car door and shifted, ready to step her strong leg out first.

"Have you ever been? Figured it'd be good for you, since you seem to be a little strung-out lately," Lexi said on the way into the building.

Courtney shook her head, and as stoked as she was with the idea, she wondered how effective her aim would be if she had crutches holding her upright. "Have you?" she asked instead.

Lexi held the door open for her, and as Courtney stepped over the threshold and into the building, the amount of people inside had her hesitating. "Think I'm the one of the few in Vancouver who's never been to the range," she muttered, not exactly loving the thought of shooting a gun for the first time with a crowd watching. Had she'd known she'd reach this point in her life where firing one sounded damn exciting, she'd have thought to ask Kris for lessons ages ago.

Completely unnerved by the crowd, and seemingly oblivious to the few in the room checking Courtney out, Lexi led her by the elbow to the registration desk. After they filled out a waiver form, retrieved their safety gear, and selected the handgun they'd use — a semiautomatic, much like the ones often in the movies — she followed Lexi to another room.

"You'll wanna wear these, beautiful girl," she said, lifting one of the sets of ear protection in her hands.

"Had I known where we were headed, I would've stopped home to change first," Courtney told her, resting on the crutches and holding out her hand. Instead of passing the ear protection to her, Lexi crooked a finger under her chin and dropped a lingering kiss on Courtney's lips.

"If you'd have known, you would've distracted me with sex instead." She gave Courtney a knowing look before fitting the earmuffs onto her head. She put her own on, and together they entered the range. People of all ages were behind the firing line, and for a moment Courtney stopped to watch as a teen fired her pistol in rapid succession at her paper target.

"Dayum," she breathed, seeing all the head and chest shots in the target.

Lexi touched her arm, gesturing to the empty booth down the line. "C'mon," she said before heading away from her. Courtney hobbled to catch up, and when they reached their designated firing stall, she watched as Lexi set the gun down on the counter. She pulled out a box of ammunition she'd put in her jacket pocket earlier, setting that down as well.

Courtney cleared her throat, and the aggressive lust rolling through her as she watched Lexi eject the magazine wasn't lost on her. Fuckin' fuck, she needed to get laid, and *fast.* "How, um ... how long have you been doing this?" She couldn't even think straight.

Lexi glanced up from fishing the ammunition into the magazine, catching Courtney's gaze. She picked the gun up and smoothly slid in the magazine, like she'd been doing it forever. "My pops used to take me and my brothers. We all know how to shoot; actually, the brother you didn't meet is on the force back home." Aiden Cole; she'd seen pictures on the mantel in her living room of Lexi's half-brother. A little less handsome, a whole lot more rugged, and married with four kids.

Lexi stripped off her leather jacket and hung it on the coat hook before she gently guided Courtney in front. It wasn't a big space by any means, and Courtney found herself leaning her crutches off to the side. That was okay, because Lexi quickly became flush with her body, thereby taking on some of her weight. Her hands slid slowly down Courtney's arms, and if she didn't know any better, she'd have thought Lexi was getting her riled up on purpose.

"Pick up the Glock." Her breath fanned Courtney's neck as she dealt out instructions.

Courtney shivered, doing as she was told. The gun felt strange in her hand, cool and slick and yet not too heavy. It also felt nice, as if holding it was somehow giving her a kickass power she didn't already have. She supposed it was true in a way; she could've easily killed Dobie that day had she been carrying. She could have saved Drew, instead of watching the scene play out like a fucking helpless damsel. Going to prison to keep Drew alive would have been worth it.

She tightened her hold on the Glock, turning it over in her hand, careful not to slip her finger in the trigger guard. "Good, beautiful girl. Now flick off the safety with your free hand, and then place both hands on the grip to shoot," Lexi continued to explain. Courtney watched her hit the button on the wall to send the target down and away.

"It's awkward with your leg, but try to arch your frame forward some and steady your arms out in front of you. The better balance you have, the easier it'll be to shoot."

Courtney did as Lexi suggested, but all her movements felt wrong, and she couldn't figure out if the issue was her stance or her arms. Lexi's hands came around her waist, silently guiding Courtney's hips back so they were flush with one another. Then her fingers were sliding down Courtney's arms to grasp her hands still holding the gun.

"You'll wanna slacken your left arm at the elbow, like this," Lexi instructed, her lips close to Courtney's muffled ear and her body just altogether too close for any amount of concentration. Lexi's breasts pressed against the back of Courtney's blouse, and all she could think about for a second was how firm Lexi's nipples must have been for her to feel them through two shirts.

Who the fuck did she need to shoot in order to get Lexi naked? 'Cause she'd do it; the moments were rare these days and becoming un-fucking-bearable.

The sound and feel of the bullet ejecting from the chamber snapped Courtney's attention back to the firing lane. "Fuuuuck," she exclaimed, giddy laughter bubbling out of her as she realized she'd somehow gotten her finger on the trigger and pulled. Talk about bringing a fantasy to life!

Her pulse was racing, her nerve endings energized like she'd just been powered up. Hot damn, she needed to do that again. She looked at her target, Dobie's ugly mug flashing through her mind like a fucking trauma trigger before she fired. She might not be able to kill him for real, but damn if she couldn't try through her thoughts.

Lexi's hands closed over hers, effectively pulling her away from her bloodthirst, and she realized the trigger was emptily clinking now. She was trembling, her breaths ragged. She found herself dying for the chance to corner Dobie.

"That's it, beautiful girl. Let yourself feel every fucked-up emotion," Lexi called. She slipped the gun out of Courtney's slack grasp and popped out the magazine to reload, all the while continuing to have Courtney against her for support. Lexi was ... well, pretty fucking exceptional, if Courtney was being honest.

She watched Lexi hit the return button and blushed when they both gaped at the target. Out of all the shots fired, only one landed, straight between the eyes. Lexi grinned. "Wonder if that was the first or the last bullet?"

A slow grin teased the corners of Courtney mouth, and then she laughed. She felt *amazing,* raw and free and brutal all at the same time. She reached for the gun. "Think this might be as good a release as sex."

"Figured you'd say something like that."

Courtney turned in Lexi's arms and planted an appreciative kiss to her lips. Their eyes met, and the softness in Lexi's didn't immediately make Courtney falter. For having such a promiscuous track record of bedding women, Lexi seemed to have eyes only for Courtney when they were together.

She kissed her again, her lips lingering for a moment before she murmured, not even sure she'd be heard in the loud room. "Thank you for this, Lex. I'll never forget it."

Chapter 21

Kitsilano Cemetery, May 21

"LIFE IS SO MUCH harder without you," she whispered miserably as she stared down at Drew's tombstone. The weather was perfect today, the fresh spring scent and blooming flowers giving life to their otherwise dead surroundings. If Drew were alive, she'd have been taking pictures everywhere she turned. "I'm trying, baby girl; I am. I'm home, facing everything that happened. Lexi, she's ... unexpected, but I kind of think you already know." Courtney snickered. She could totally see Drew trying to match-make up in Heaven, or wherever people went when they died. She thought of the letter she'd received the day before from Katie, glad she was again in a financial state where she could help her new friend and the kids. They'd reached Saskatchewan and were currently hiding out using an alias. She'd told Lexi about them, but only because she'd walked in on Courtney reading the letter. She wondered if Lexi was still asleep in Courtney's bed. It was going on ten, but Lexi would easily sleep until noon if she didn't have to work. She was going home tomorrow but had offered to go with Courtney to see Kris again.

She sniffled, wiping at her eyes and studying Drew's tombstone. She licked her dry lips, saying hoarsely, "I loved you so much, and I know you loved me the best way you could, but..." Her voice trailed off; she had to clear her throat before she could continue. "I only wish you'd been in love with me instead of Kris. I could've made you happy, Drew. We could've ... I dunno, had kids of our own or something. Whatever you wanted, I would've done everything to help you get it."

A soft laugh escaped her, and she waved her hand to shoo away the fantasy. "I don't say it to make you feel bad. You know I hate when you're upset. I'm just saying — if we'd been a couple, then you might still be here. But then I guess we wouldn't have Cadence, and damn, she's the sweetest kid, baby girl. You would be so proud of her.

"I've thought long and hard about it, and I'm not going to fight anymore. I thought you should be the first to know. I'm already waking up with stiff joints not associated with my broken leg, so getting beat up is taking a toll on me. I–I just think of me in the future, you know? Do I want to be healthy like I am now, or do I wanna be in a wheelchair or using a cane 'cause I fucked up my knees or back?" She chewed her lip, adding, "It makes the most sense, and besides, I'm tired of craving the rush. I want to see if I can learn to appreciate the slow lane. I know I did when I was with you, but it's a bitch by myself. When I slow down too much, I find myself thinking, and it gets to me, you know? It gets to me. But I want to change, Drew. I don't want you disappointed in who I've become."

She glanced over her shoulder at Rita, who stood a few feet away, two bouquets in her arms. "Rita, do you mind? Thank you."

Rita nodded, coming up beside her and bending to place the flowers in the vases around Drew's gravestone. "*Descansa en paz*, Drew. *Tu siempre fuiste una niña dulce. Yo ame tus galletas de chocolate.*"

Courtney smiled at her housekeeper and lifelong companion. She was so frigging cute, it was almost criminal to be that nice. "Rita's here, baby girl. She says rest in peace, and that you were always sweet, and she loved your chocolate chip cookies."

When Rita moved away so Courtney could be alone once more, she knew it was time to say what she'd come to say. "I haven't forgotten your last demand, Drew. It's doable, if I open myself up enough. I can't promise you the outcome you want, but I promise I'll try. I'll try to love Kris and Cadence with everything I've got, because that's exactly how I loved you. With my whole heart and soul, forever."

THANK YOU FOR TAKING the time to read Cage Me! Please consider leaving a review to help other readers experience this whirlwind journey! It helps more than you know!

Want more of Courtney, Kris, and Lexi? Pre-order *Hate Me* to read about Kris in his sole POV debut!

Join the Facebook reader group here: <u>Angel's Bad A$$ Readers</u>

Flip ahead for a sneak peek!

Want more? Check out this deleted scene from the book!

From Angel

Cage Me has been the best experience (so far!) I could ever have given myself as a writer. Courtney's journey through the metaphoric battlefield of loss and love has shown me the kind of person I strive to be every day. *Cage Me* has taught me that life is fucked-up for everyone, in varying degrees, and don't be so quick to tap out of the fight. You get knocked down, get back up again; you bleed, make them bleed harder. Never be a victim.

I can only hope you fall in love with Courtney as I have. I'm on the sidelines just as you are, cheering her on and exuberantly waiting the day she gets her HEA! Until then, I guess I'll be finding out what kind of shit Kris can stir up!

Spread joy!

Angel

About the Author

Angel Jendrick is the author of gritty contemporary romances. She's also been known to dabble in poetry from time to time. When not writing or editing (or thinking about writing or editing), she can be found watching movies, jamming to her favorite tunes, running after her kids, or working on her latest home reno or DIY project.

Angel lives in Canada on thirteen beautiful acres of land with her wife, their three children, Ellie their energetic lab and a blind cat name Taz.

She is currently working on the final two books in her Claiming Kristopher series.

Tune into the *Cage Me* playlist on Spotify!

Sign up for Angel Jendrick's *newsletter*:
https://landing.mailerlite.com/webforms/landing/h9g6l2
Follow Angel at the links below!
https://www.facebook.com/angeljendrick/
https://www.instagram.com/angeljendrickauthor/
https://www.goodreads.com/author/show/16171551.Angel_Jendrick
https://twitter.com/angeljendrick
https://www.tiktok.com/@angeljendrick
https://www.bookbub.com/authors/angel-jendrick
www.angeljendrick.com

Acknowledgments

Thanks to everyone who made *Cage Me* possible. My editors Colleen and Allister; my proof reader Mim; my alpha and beta readers, Amanda, Connie, Vanessa, and Jayne; my cover designer, Quinn. Thank you so much! You took my baby and cranked up its awesomeness!

Special thanks to my amigo Rafael Aguirre for your knowledge of the Spanish language. Much appreciated!

Thanks to my family for the support this past year. Life with you guys is a blessing I won't take for granted.

Thanks to Jaclyn, Cara, and Andrea for checking in and never forgetting about me while I lose myself in the story.

To YOU. Even if I could do this without you, it wouldn't be nearly as fun and worthwhile. So thank you!! I'm stoked that other people love Kris and the gang as much as I do.

Stay tuned for *Hate Me*!

Hate Me Sneak Peek

KRIS FIRST BECAME AWARE of water raining down his scarred back, and then slick hands slithering down his right arm to slowly pry open his wounded hand. Distinct vision returned seconds before recognition seeped into his foggy senses.

"The fuck? What the actual fuck!" he cried, though the raspiness in his voice made the exclamation sound more like gibberish than anything.

He was sitting on some kind of bathtub chair in a large shower with the spray indeed wetting his hair and back. A woman stood on his left, holding the handheld nozzle as she washed soap from his curls, and a dude was washing his fucking biceps. Both had medical gloves on and were acting completely professional, but none of that mattered because Kris's one rule of thumb came on front and centre in his mind.

Strangers were *not* allowed to touch him.

An invisible hand closed around his throat, effectively cutting off his air as he grappled with reality. He had no control over the hand raising up to shove the woman into the shower wall. The other man in the tiny space glanced to him in shock before he got Kris's fist in the gut. He was weak as fuck, so the desired impact was lacking, but it shoved the dude off long enough for Kris to pull himself off the chair.

His legs wobbled around in slow motion before collapsing from under him. He groaned as he landed face-first onto the wet tile. The discomfort in his dick was immediate, and then relief came as he felt piss run hot down his leg. "So weak," he muttered, fear settling in the pit of his stomach as he realized he couldn't run from them. He was utterly at their mercy, butt fucking naked with his legs sprawled out.

The woman crouched down in front of his head, and he could barely make out her gentle words over the roaring in his ears. His breaths were shallow now, people around him fuzzy as he tried to take in air.

"...you hear me? Kris, you're in a care facility. We've been bathing you once a week for over a year. You're completely safe with us, I promise."

"Damn, I think he pulled the catheter out," the guy behind him said. A towel was draped over him a moment later.

"I wanna see my girls," he heard himself wheeze. A hand shot out and grabbed the woman's arm like he was asthmatic and in desperate need of a puffer. Their eyes collided, and the raw sympathy in hers confused his muddled understanding. "Drew, Cadence. I wanna see them. Please, I need to talk to Drew."

"Let's get you dried off and dressed, and then I'll get in touch with Dr. Matheson or Ms. Cairns, okay? I'm sure they'd love to hear you're alert. And the doctors on your case will need to be notified."

Dr. Matheson or Ms. Cairns? He struggled to sit up and couldn't remember where all his strength went. "What are you talking about, woman? Fuck sakes, you deaf? I gotta see my girls, yo!" Was he doing pills again? Is this why he was in a ... what had she called it? A care facility? Had Drew discovered and then thrown him out to these people?

"Kris, I'm sorry..."

"Let me see Drew! I wanna fucking see her *now!*"

Also By Angel Jendrick

www.ingramcontent.com/pod-product-compliance
Lightning Source LLC
Chambersburg PA
CBHW030931060726
47591CB00005B/1753